CHAPTERONE

$\mathcal{B}$est friend. Go ahead—look it up in the dictionary. Right next to it in the definition section will be one simple word: *Bitch.*

It's never a good idea to let them set you up on a date—especially when you've been known to break out in hives at the mention of the d-word.

See those red bumps at the back of my neck? Yeah, those little bastards have been hanging around ever since she called three days ago and said she'd found me a date.

I threatened to vomit. I still w*ant* to vomit. I don't date. I'm not a dater. And not for some bullshit reason like I got my heart broken or I'm a commitment-phobe or I was cheated on. No—I'm single because I want to be. I don't date because I don't want to—mostly because I have no desire to wipe pee off my toilet seat.

It is literally that simple.

Except… It isn't. Not quite.

I'm a serial one-nighter. A hitter and a quitter. A whammer, bammer, thank you mammer.

And yes, I am the proud owner of a vagina with the female reproductive organs, and I also happen to have a banging pair of tits.

What? If I can't appreciate them, no one else will.

In the last three years, I've slept with exactly thirty-six men. I've seen one of them more than once, but it was such a booty call and so draining that I ended that crap quicker than Mr. Tap-Tap-Squirt, my sexually enthusiastic neighbor. I've mistaken his escapades for a knock on my front door more than once.

One time, I even knocked back through the wall in case he was communicating with Morse code. That was awkward. Especially when he showed up in nothing but his robe.

His pink robe. I'd hoped at the time it was his date's, but I've since seem him proudly taking the trash out since then.

"Come on, Bee," pleads Charlotte "Charley" Hill, my best friend, bracing her hands on her hips. She's towering above me, standing tall in a pretty hot pair of heels. She looks like she's ready to go give the pole the time of its life down at the local strip club.

"Nope." I ignore the dress and heels she's set on the sofa opposite me. I look like I haven't showered in a week—although I did so this morning before work—and I'm slouched on the sofa in a manner worthy of a teenaged body waiting for his porn movie to buffer.

All hail sweatpants.

"Come on. He's been dragged to this, too. He hates dating. You're kindred spirits."

I snort. "So send him round with beer and wine and we'll skip the date part of the night."

"You're so boring, do you know that?"

I shove a tortilla chip into some salsa and pause, skirting my gaze toward her. "I'm not boring, Charley. I'm simply self-serving. Look at this—if I dated, would I be able to lie here on my sofa, feet on the coffee table, nomming down chips like I don't care about my muffin top, while wearing yesterday's bra?"

"When you put it like that, you really need to date."

Shrugging, I shove the chip into my mouth and chew, staring intently at her.

With a sigh, she presses her hands together in front of her. Then, putting her hands back on her hips, she looks at the ceiling. Her lips move slowly as she silently counts to three, and then, "Right, that's it, Bee Donnelly! I'm officially staging an intervention!"

"I don't need a—hey, bring that back!" I lunge for the bowl of chips she swipes from the table and fall to my knees. "Charley! Don't be a bitch!"

She slams the bowl down on the kitchen counter and a few chips fly out. She turns, her hands back on her hips, her dark eyes blazing. "No. I don't give a shit if this is the only damn date you go on this year. I've gone to the trouble of organizing this, and you're gonna go on it!"

"You just said he was forced into it too," I point out, kneeling back. "You're not fucking cupid."

Charley storms across to the other sofa, grabs the dress and heels, and shoves them at me. "I might not be cupid, but I know how to use these shoes as weapons. Take them and get changed." She pushes them into my chest and drags me to my feet.

Jesus, for a short chick, she's strong.

"I hate you."

"I know, Bee. But you might get laid at the end of the night. We'll talk then."

I grasp the bundle of items tightly and storm into my room. Goddamn it. Having a serial dater for a best friend is not fucking working out for me. I might have to cut her ass loose. So what if we've been best friends since we were four?

BLIND DATE

EMMA HART

New York Times Bestselling Author

bl

ii

BLIND DATE

a novella

For everyone who asked for more of Bee and Carter.
It's not much, but I hope it's enough. Thank you for loving them more than I thought you would.
This one is for you.

We're not four and we can't both have the same Barbie house for Christmas. She wants to date. Fine. She can date. Let her date her pretty way through Mr. Asshole, Sir Cheat-a-Lot, and Lord Pencil-Dick.

I'll be quite happy to skip the date and hop straight to the bedroom with Mr. Cock Piercing, Sir Pussy-Eater, and Lord Multiple-Orgasm.

Just not at the same time.

Although. Sir Pussy-Easter and Lord Multiple-Orgasm could be on to something there.

"Bee!" Charley bangs on my bedroom door. "I hope you're getting changed."

I open the door and throw yesterday's bra in her face.

Bitch.

———◦◦◦◦———

"I really fucking hate you."

"Damn, they aren't even here yet and you hate me *that* much?"

I roll my eyes and take a sip of my wine. My narrowed eyes scan the restaurant, and I shift in my seat. I'm not comfortable in this dress in the slightest. It feels way too much like it's a day job dress. If you ignore the sleeves that are slightly off-shoulder and the fact my mom would fire me if I turned up with a dress this short. At least my boobs are covered. I guess.

"How much longer do we have to wait? My stomach is contemplating digesting itself." I lean over slightly and close the gap between our small, square tables.

"I just remembered why you don't date. You're so rude."

I glare at her, but she's grinning. Bitch. "Look, I'm hungry. You took away my chips."

"Are you twenty-six or a toddler?"

"Depends on the day and what I'm doing. When I'm eating, I'm a toddler. Always."

"Well can we revert back to being twenty-six now? Because they're here."

"Who are they? The mafia? The Avengers?"

"Bee," she growls, discreetly slapping the side of my thigh with the back of her fingers.

I just about refrain from rolling my eyes again and release my vice-like grip on my wine glass. Play nice, Bee. That's all you have to do. For ninety minutes at least.

"Bee," Charley says, "This is Carter Hughes."

Great. Here we go.

I place my hands on the table and push up to standing. And, shit.

Holy.

Fucking.

Shit.

Dear God, did you send Carter Hughes as a beautiful treat for me? Is it because I finalized the mother of all contracts at work this week?

Because thank you. Thank. Fucking. *You.*

His dark hair is cut short, and it's slightly longer along the middle and spiked in an odd kind of Mohawk way, but the rest of his hair is just long enough that it doesn't look stupid. In fact, it's kind of swept to the side, too. But who the hell am I kidding—I'm not focusing on that hair. I'm focusing on everything that is his face.

His eyes—holy fucking ovary boom. They're the most startling bright green I've ever seen. They're almost emerald in their intensity, and the intensity is spine-shivering in the best kind of way. His eyes are crawling over me slowly, every tiny spark flaring in those captivating irises firing a bolt of attraction and desire my way.

It's also how his mouth curves to the side that has his cheek quirking, revealing a tiny dimple on that cheek, the only so-called blemish on his perfectly smooth skin.

And his mouth. We won't go there with his God-given perfectly pink lips and his expert turn upward.

"It's a pleasure to meet you, Ms. Donnelly," he says, his voice husky as he takes my hand. He lifts it to his mouth and brushes his lips warmly across my knuckles.

"I'd love to say the pleasure is all mine," I muse, admiring the way that suit hugs his shoulders, "but I'm sure I might be lying."

Carter Hughes stops, his mouth hovering against my fingers, and smiles. "That you might."

"And the name is Bee," I add as an afterthought.

Yes, sir. My name sure is Bee. You can try it on later.

"Bee," he murmurs. "As in the animal?"

"As in the animal," I agree. *Damn hippie father.* I half-smile, ignoring the shivers that cascade across my skin when his fingers clasp around mine. He shakes my hand. The movement is easy and slow, but his grip is tight and strong, and his thumb flexes as it brushes across mine just a little too harshly.

Hello, Mr. Hughes. I declare that you're interested.

"Does the name reflect the personality?" He quirks a brow, slowly, and the easy way his lips curve into a smirk has my stomach flipping.

"As in bright with a sharp tongue?" I curve my eyebrow upward to match his.

"Wouldn't you like to know, Mr. Hughes?"

His grip on mine tightens, and he pulls me toward him. It's hard enough that I have to step forward to keep my balance. "Absolutely," he responds. "I have sixty minutes of this little slice of hell before I'm out of here. Convince me to stay longer."

Sixty minutes. Excellent. Thirty less than I'd planned for.

I brush my finger down the center of his stomach, its smooth journey interrupted by the bump of his button. "I would… except I have no interest in drawing this out any longer than it needs to be. Looks like you're stuck to sixty minutes of my stunning company." I smile sweetly, pat his deliciously firm stomach, and step back.

"Really," he drawls, grasping the back of my chair as I sit and pushing me in. "Stunning—is that the personality or the looks?"

"I'd love to tell you, but where's the fun in that?" I follow him with my eyes as he takes the seat opposite me. "You'll just have to find out for yourself."

He drops his head as he sits, but those startling green eyes raise beneath thick, dark lashes to meet mine. "Can I get you another drink, Ms. Donnelly?"

"Not as long as you continue to call me Ms. Donnelly."

"Bee," he corrects himself, his lips quirking again. "A nickname?"

"Unfortunately not," I reply. "My father was… eccentric."

He smiles as he waves a confident hand in the general direction of a server. "Red or white?"

"Blush."

"Clearly the stunning part of your previous statement wasn't your personality," he teases, turning to the server. "A bottle of your finest blush wine for the lady, and I'll have your best merlot. Thank you."

"A bottle, Mr. Hughes? Are you trying to get me drunk?"

"Will you stay longer than an hour?"

"Absolutely not."

He leans forward, resting his forearms on the table. "I'll ask you after another glass." He grins, and it's playful, an endearingly charming smile.

I'd bet he uses that on all the girls.

I curl my fingers around the stem of my wine glass, swirl the small amount of pink liquid left, and drink it in one. "And my answer will be the same."

An hour in the restaurant, I mean. If he felt like taking it outside would be proactive, I'd be down with that. This man is fucking fine. And by fine, I mean he's fucking *fah-ha-hiiiiine.*

"What do you do?" I ask, acknowledging the server with a tilt of my head as he fills my glass. Halfway. Professional, but ridiculous. Wine glasses should be full at all times.

"I work in business," Carter Hughes answers. "And you?"

"I also work in business, along with one hundred percent of working Americans."

"You're kind of sassy, you know that?"

"Kind of? No, sir. I'm incredibly sassy. I'm just handing it to you in small doses so you don't get overwhelmed." Another sweet smile.

"Bee," he says it in a low voice, leaning toward me, his glass raised to his lips. "If you think it's your sass that's overwhelming, you haven't looked in the mirror."

"Well, that's sweet, isn't it?"

"And true."

"That's what they all say." I pause. "Are you trying to get in my panties? Because it's a little early, don't you think?"

"For sex?" He takes one long, slow drink, his eyes never wavering on me. "It's never too early for sex."

Huh. We agree on that, then. "Unless that sex is the morning after when one of you should have left in the middle of the night."

Carter's lips move slowly, oh so slowly, into a smile that is equal parts amused and predatory. A thrill runs down my spine—and I know why. It's cat and mouse.

The chase.

It's starting.

"Oh, Bee," he mutters. Darkly. So, so darkly. "Could it be that I'm finally on a date with someone that understands my aversion to that commitment bullshit?"

"Please don't use the 'c' word in my presence. It makes me sick."

His eyes flash with a hint of desire. "You know, I find myself not hungry at all. Shall we move this conversation into the bar?"

"Great idea," I say, grabbing my wine glass, then my purse from the back of the chair.

He lifts his hand, waves, and a server appears as if by magic. "Can you have this wine bottle moved through to booth one and have my usual on the table? Thank you."

I raise one eyebrow as he stands, the server smoothly removing the wine bucket from the table and heading out through a door. Hell, I didn't even know this restaurant had a separate bar area, never mind booths.

Carter holds out his hand, his fingers stretched toward me. "Shall we?"

Ignoring my best friend's eyes on me, I place my smaller hand in his and stand. "You seem to know this place well," I comment casually, taking a step in front of him.

His hand finds its way to the small of my back, and he leans in so his lips brush my ear. His breath coasts across my cheek in a thick swath of warmth. "Bee, I own this restaurant."

"And I'm assuming it was your intention to bring every date to it," I say dryly.

"On the contrary, I do my best to avoid dates and my business. However, I was tied to this by my buddy's insistence of having this, and his date's insistence on it being a double. My restaurant was, naturally, the only one that could free two tables at such short notice."

Ah. I knew Charley was a dirty liar. Her date just happened to have a single friend my ass. "How very convenient for you."

"Is it? Does the fact I own this building bother you?"

"Why would it? All I know about you is that your name is Carter Hughes, you want to get me drunk because it isn't too early for sex, and you own this fine establishment." I turn so I'm walking backward, and careful of my glass, grasp the lapel of his jacket. "Honey, I won't remember your name tomorrow morning, let alone the rest of that. So, no, you can say it doesn't bother me at all."

We move into a seating area that's darker than the restaurant. The only lighting is really from the bar area. It's all black marble and black leather seating here, from the stools lining up along the glass bar to the cushioned booth seating. And it's all couples—two people to a booth, despite the fact each one could easily sit six. Each one is curtained, too. Translucent black curtains cover the openings, and Carter tightens his grip on me as he reaches for one of them.

"Take a seat," he breathes into my ear.

Okay.

I slip past him and drop myself on the seat. "This is… different."

"The bar area is… exclusive," he explains, slowly. "It's invite only. Otherwise no one would be able to get a booth."

"And this one? Is yours?" I look around it. There's a tiny light on the wall, casting an eerily sensual feeling across the small area. The circular table in front of me is just big enough to hold two plates of food, a wine bucket, and a glass or two.

I get the feeling not much eating happens here, though. Unless that eating happens to be a pussy or a cock.

My clit throbs. Is this why he brought me here?

Of course it is, Bee. It's why you came, you stupid bitch.

"Always," Carter finally answers my question. He pulls the wine bottle from the bucket, shakes it lightly, then tops up my glass. The ice clinks as he replaces the bottle and reaches for his small tumbler full of amber liquid. It looks like liquid gold in this light. "There are ten booths. Next to you could be a Hollywood

7

sweetheart, a billionaire, a world-famous model… Who knows? I don't even know. It's not my business to know."

"It's not your business to know about your business?" My lips tug into a small smirk.

His eyes seem to glow as he focuses on me. "I have my own perks within my business. I wouldn't have brought you back here if I didn't think you weren't interested in them."

I cross one leg over the other, grab my glass, and lean back. "Tell me—what are your perks, Mr. Hughes?"

He flexes his finger against his glass and brings it upward. "My perk, *Ms. Donnelly,* is wondering how many times I can make you come before I fuck you."

Heat sizzles through my bloodstream, and goosebumps cover my skin in the silence that follows his words.

Holy. Shit.

That's forward.

And tempting. Oh so goddamn, motherfucking tempting.

"That's awfully presumptuous," I manage to rasp out. I take a quick gulp of wine to wet my throat. "Don't you think?"

"I'm a presumptuous guy." He shrugs a shoulder, unaffected.

Of course. "What makes you think you're going to find out?"

He moves his gaze over me slowly, his eyes darkening with every inch of my skin they touch. My heartbeat picks up until it's thundering against my ribs and I can feel the beat at every pulse point in my body. There's a tightening sensation in my stomach that seems to be dropping and resting deep in my pussy, and I'm clenching my muscles, and I wish that awkward ache in my clit would disappear, because I kind of want to jump Carter's bones right now.

He chuckles, the sound dark and husky, and sets his glass on the table after one final drink. "Oh, Bee." He skirts across the seat toward me, and I take a deep breath when he reaches up and loosens his tie. "I know I'm going to find out," he says just as darkly as he just laughed. "Look at you. You're breathing erratically." He runs his finger across my collarbone and glances toward the table. "Your hand is trembling where you're holding your glass, and you keep licking those gorgeous lips of yours." He trails his hand up my neck. "Not to mention your eyes —they're wide, and your cheeks are flushed." He cups my jaw and runs his thumb along the side of it, right down to my mouth. The tip of his thumb ghosts along the soft curve of my lower lip. He's barely touching me, but it feels as though my mouth is on fire.

He leans in, the tip of his nose only just hovering in front of mine, and he exhales slowly. His breath cascades across my mouth, and I breathe in sharply at the hot burst of air that caresses my lips.

Oh, Jesus.

"Are you wondering yet?" he whispers. "Tell me, Bee. Are you wondering how many times I could make you come? How I'd do it? I am. All I'm thinking about right now is lifting the bottom of your dress, sliding your underwear to the side and fucking you with my fingers until you bite down on my shoulder with pleasure."

Another burst of heat is making its way through my body. I clamp my thighs together as he drops one hand and draws a trail across my left leg with the tips of his fingers. "I'm thinking that I should leave," I lie.

"No you're not." He smiles and spreads his hand across my thigh. I fight to keep my muscles clenched and ultimately lose. Carter inches his hand up my leg until his fingers tease the hem of my dress and his thumb pushes between my legs. He squeezes my thigh, and unbidden, my legs creep open.

I breathe faster with anticipation, each one harder and more desperate as his hand continues its journey upward. I drop my head back as he finally reaches the very top of my thigh. His thumb brushes across my panties, and I don't know if the gentle flick across my clit is deliberate or coincidental, but I shudder.

He drops his face into my neck, repeating that flick. Yeah—that was deliberate. And I hate how good it feels. He smiles against my skin, pushing down hard. The lace of my panties rubs against the sensitive spot roughly, but it only adds to the pleasure, the crazy, intense, burst of pleasure that ricochets as he circles my clit with his thumb.

Oh, God. I'm such a slut. I've barely known this man thirty minutes and he's just slid two of his fingers inside me.

He groans, the sound muffled by my collarbone. "You're so fucking wet, Bee. Still gonna lie and tell me you think you should leave?"

I open my mouth to respond as he pumps his fingers inside me, but nothing comes out. Instead, I swallow and nod, even as my hips move against his hand.

Greedy pussy. Bad pussy.

I am so grounding her tomorrow morning.

Carter slips his thumb under my panties until it touches my bare clit. His fingers still for the barest second as he finds the sweet spot and settles there, ready to move again. Blood is pumping through my body at lightning speed, and my fingers are wrapped in his jacket, and I'm grasping the seat, digging my nails into the leather as he moves his hand again. My legs are opening wider with each thrust of his fingers into me. His lips skirt their way across my neck, up to my ear and back down, kissing, nibbling, brushing… It's a sensory overload.

With one final rub of my clit, he pushes me over the edge.

Orgasm one.

CHAPTERTWO

I moan, and he covers my mouth with his hand, still moving the other against me. I ride the orgasm out against his hand, trembles of the aftershocks of it going through my body. "Holy shit," I whisper, the words leaving me on a whoosh. The man hasn't even kissed me. At least, not on my mouth.

I've never been turned on so easily in my life.

Carter pulls his fingers out of my pussy and grasps my hip. His grip is tight, and when he pulls me toward him, I move onto my side. I unclip the button of his jacket, and looking down at his stomach, flatten my hand against the toned surface of his body. Damn that crisp white shirt stopping me from touching his skin. Abs just aren't the fucking same when they've got a damn row of buttons running down the middle of them.

Carter wraps one hand around the back of my neck and pulls my face into him. "God, Bee. You get wet so easily, don't you? Is that how you keep your one-nighters going? With your wet pussy?" He leans in so his fingers dig into my pulse point. "How long do you last?" he asks quietly. "One? Two? Three? Tell me, love. How many times can you come before it's too much? Before you say enough is enough?"

"Once." I rasp out the word, gripping his shirt tightly.

"You're a liar," he replies, just as breathily. He palms my ass cheek, his movements slow and calculated. I hold my breath in anticipation of the sting I know is coming.

It does.

Sharp and quick, Carter's palm connects with my ass cheek, and I buck my hips against him.

"Fuck," I moan, gripping his shirt tighter.

He laughs. Low and rich, each sound coasts over my skin until all I can hear is that deep rumble of his amusement. "Sounds like a good fuck." He does it again, and this time, I arch my back. "Damn. You're so fuckin' responsive, aren't you?"

"You've barely touched me," I point out. I reach up and grasp the top button of his shirt, my eyes on his the whole time. "See how responsive I am when you actually try."

Once again, he laughs. His grip on my tender ass gets rough, and he seems to relish the way I grasp his shirt as if I want to rip it off. 'Cause, fuck. I do. I want to rip off this goddamn useless piece of white fucking fabric until his obviously toned torso is clear to me and ready for me to explore with whichever part of my body I deem fit.

Ah, fuck it.

I undo the top button, then another, and another, and another. My fingers travel down nimbly until every one of the little white buttons are undone and only the very bottom of his shirt is tucked into his waistband. I run my teeth across my bottom lip, deliberately pulling tightly on the soft flesh. His grip does nothing but tighten, so I move, hooking one leg over his lap until I'm straddling him.

I can feel his rock-hard cock pushing against my already wet pussy, and fuck me. That's one hell of a cock.

I rock my hips against him, and when a small groan leaves him, I smile. I'll take it. I take whatever inch of pleasure I can, given that he just sucked it from me. No arguments here, but damn.

Maybe Carter Hughes needs a taste of his own medicine.

My lips quirk to one side at the prospect.

I've barely known him an hour, but I want to see what he can do with his cock when it's compromised by a chick's mouth.

I lean back, drop my hands to his belt, and pause when his hover against me.

"Server," he murmurs, curling his arm around me and pulling me into him. I turn my face a fraction toward the curtains. The server is standing there, her eyes trained on the area above his head.

"Same again," he replies, holding me where I am until the woman has left again. The second the curtains close, he twines my hair around his fingers and tugs me face toward his so tightly that my breath catches. "You think you're so fucking smart, don't you? Baby, my cock is hard for you. Feel it." He takes my hand and pushes it onto his erection. "If you're gonna suck it, get your mouth the fuck down there and suck it before that bitch comes back with our drinks."

Holy. Did he really just refer to a member of his staff as a bitch?

He did.

He did.

Oh my God.

I shouldn't do this. I should run like fuck. But, damn. I wanna know what that sweet, hard cock tastes like, even if it's only just one taste. I want to know what it's like to have his pleasure pulsing against my tongue…. What it's like to have this powerful man entirely at my mercy.

So I do it.

I push the table away from us the smallest amount and grab his undone pants. My fingers curl around each side and I tug them down until he lifts his ass and his sharp, black pants slide down his muscular thighs easily.

"Bee…" he warns, his hands both sliding up my back to the back of my head.

"Carter," I murmur, grabbing the waistband of his boxer briefs, taking the barest moment to appreciate the way his hardened cock is pushing against the thin fabric of his underwear. It's like a fucking oil painting, worthy of being hung in any art museum.

He tenses as I tug down his boxers and his cock springs free, long, hard, and thick, with a vein pulsing along its side.

I grin.

Time to play.

I close my mouth around the head of his cock, touching the tip of my tongue to it. He groans and twines his hand in my hair, tugging lightly. His restraint is obvious. Wrapping my fingers around the bottom of his cock, I give him a gentle squeeze as I take him in my mouth fully.

His grip on my hair tightens as I work him with both my mouth and my hand. He grows even harder in my mouth, and as I run my tongue over that one vein, I can feel it pulsing.

God, he really does have a wonderful cock.

My pussy is throbbing at the thought of having it inside me. It's almost tempting to stop this and climb on top of him.

"Your drinks, sir."

Carter holds my head still, his cock buried in my mouth. "On the table," he demands.

I massage the very tip of it with my tongue, and his hips jerk into me.

"Today," he grinds out as I reach down to cup his balls. I lightly drag my nails over them. "Don't disturb us again."

Two beats pass with the swish of a curtain before he grasps my hair so tightly that my scalp stings. He yanks my head up and meets my eyes. His gaze is dark and stormy, and it sends thrills of desire through me.

"You." It's a growl—deep, rich, primitive.

It's all he says as he grabs me and throws me back onto the chair, thankfully releasing my hair. Without another word, he undoes his tie and whips it off before leaning over me, the satin strip crunched into a ball in his fist.

Only now does he speak. "Your hands. Above your head." When I don't move, he leans down. "Now, Bee."

I raise an eyebrow and stare at him in defiance. *You want 'em there, you put 'em there.*

"My way it is then," he murmurs, taking my wrists in each hand and slamming them against the seat over my head. He holds them in place with one hand while he unravels his tie.

I inhale sharply as he wraps it around my wrists and secures it, the silky knot tight and unmovable. I know because I try to free my hands. Carter stops my effort with a simple yet hard squeeze.

"Keep them there," he breathes, running his eyes over my face. "Yes?"

"Yes." I part my lips in an effort to steady my breathing.

My body is on fire. My legs are trembling with the anticipation of what he's planning to do to me, and although this feels so right, I have to admit that I'm wondering what the hell I'm doing here. This is a new one, even for me.

Clearly the universe has decided that my one night stands need spicing up. Methinks the universe has been reading too many erotic novels.

Carter holds my gaze for a moment longer. He sits up, moving his hands to his shirt buttons. My chest heaves as I watch him undo each button and pull the fabric apart, revealing a toned torso from his pecs right down to the 'v' that leads to his erect cock. I run my eyes over the fine male form before me, and my fingers twitch with the urge to touch him. To trail my fingertips over every pack of muscle and inside each shadowed furrow.

He keeps his shirt on, just open, his eyes back on me, as he slides back a couple of inches. "Feet on the chair. Legs open. Let me see that pussy."

Blunt. To the point. I like it.

I do as he says, my clit aching at his words. *Gladly, Mr. Hughes.* I open my legs a little wider than necessary, and he reaches forward and grabs my ankle. He lifts it and rests it on the back of the seat, and I shift so it's more comfortable, making sure to keep my hands above my head like I promised.

Like he ordered, rather.

His green eyes drop from my face to my exposed pussy, and he bends forward. One of his fingers trails up the inside of my thigh, his touch feather-light, and I shiver.

Then he drops right down, splays his hands on the insides of my upper thighs, holds my legs firmly open, and closes his mouth over my pussy. He puts extra pressure on my clit, and I arch my back as a bolt of pleasure shoots through me. Good fucking God. His tongue is rough as it rubs over my most sensitive spot, and I cry out as the hint of an orgasm quivers through me.

Carter gets up and leans over me, and his cock teases the opening of my pussy before it settles over my clit. It only makes me squirm more. "Hush," he admonishes me. "No one here will know that you're coming except me. Your pleasure is mine and only mine. Understood?"

I suck my lower lip into my mouth and nod my response. How do you have an orgasm without screaming to the high heavens?

"Good girl," he murmurs, finally touching his lips to mine.

I can taste myself on his tongue. Tangy and vile, the taste of my pussy coats my lips from his. It's a brief touch, but it's deep. I rock my hips so his cock ghosts over my clit again and again, and I could totally get myself off by doing this. But it's tempting to lift my hips and—

His palm connects with the side of my ass in a sharp slap that makes me gasp. "I'll fuck you when I'm ready. By the time I do, you'll be begging me." He runs his lips down my neck. "How greedy is your pussy, Bee?" His hand slips between us. He grasps his cock and rubs it against my clit in slow, teasing circles. "How badly does it want my cock? What if I just slid it down like this and let it have a tiny bit? Would that make you happy?"

He does exactly what he said. The tip of his cock pushes inside my pussy, and I throw my head back. My arms bend as my whole body arches into him, desperate for the rest of him.

"Please," I breathe.

"Like this?" He pushes into me fully and I swear angels fucking sing.

"Oh god," I whisper, clenching around him.

I feel so full right now, and I swear, if he doesn't move and fuck me properly, I'm going to drop to my knees and plead. Or get up out of here and finish myself off with my vibrator at home.

Carter chuckles, and it's dark, but my skin tingles at the sound anyway. He withdraws from me in one smooth, swift movement, and immediately drops back to the position he was in just moments ago. Once again, he forces my legs open and covers my pussy with his mouth. His tongue attacks my clitoris. His moves are quick and harsh, each touch purposeful and meant to punish as well as pleasure.

I writhe on the seat, my legs trembling, as he licks the small bundle of throbbing nerves. Each bolt of happy desire that floods right through me, pounding through my bloodstream, is a teasing reminder of the pleasure that awaits me if he follows through on this orgasm.

And, hell. I hope he does.

He licks me unashamedly, devouring every inch of my aching core. My pussy muscles tense and relax as if he's still inside me, and if it weren't for the way he slides his fingers into me, I'd be able to imagine that he is. Instead, it's real. So fucking real.

Sparks erupt across my body as he lifts my legs high and opens them wider until it's almost painful for me. Fortunately, the pleasure he's creating with just the tip of his tongue and two of his fingers pumping inside of me far outweighs it. My arms ache with the desire to reach down and twine my fingers into his hair, to hold his face against me until I've come again and again and again, but the tie that strains when I try reminds me that I can't.

That I agreed to this. To be partially bound and therefore much more vulnerable to him than I would be otherwise.

And I agreed. God, why did I agree?

The orgasm hits me blindingly, and I shiver, arching my back, clenching my legs, fisting my hands, biting the inside of my cheek to keep the moan inside. I want to cry out, I want to scream. I want to tell the world that a thousand fireworks just erupted inside me.

But I can't. So I don't. I just lie here, biting my tongue, my lip, my cheek, breathing harshly until the initial wave of pleasure has passed and I'm nothing more than a puddle of person on the chair.

So. That's why I agreed.

Carter stands, slaps my legs together with a squeeze of my ass, and moves over me. Not his body, though. No—he moves his pelvis over me until his cock is brushing against my lips. Unconsciously, my mouth opens, and he pushes it into my mouth.

Here, I'm totally helpless, unable to do anything as he moves his hips and fucks my mouth until he's done. I flick my tongue and close my eyes when a tiny spurt of his semen coats my tongue with saltiness. I want to reach forward and…

It's amazing how much you rely on your hands until you can't use them anymore.

I'm totally at his mercy. The realization hits me hard. Although I could, in theory, stand and push him away from me, I don't want to. I know the magic he can work with his mouth and his fingers, and how amazing his cock feels buried deep inside me—and now I want to know what it feels like to have his cock fucking me until I can't breathe.

I don't even care how he does it.

I graze my teeth along his hard length, barely scratching his skin, and he groans. He reaches forward and grabs my hair again, and damn, I love it when he does that. I shouldn't love anything a one night stand does, but then again, I've never had this before. I've never had someone dominate me so fully.

"Fuck," he hisses when I hollow my cheeks to suck particularly hard.

The word, the tone, the breathy exhalation, the withdrawal from my mouth, it all gives me a powerful thrill.

I relish in it. The gasping undercurrent of his tone threads through my body like lightning. It gives me courage. It breeds my attitude, giving me a power I just assumed lost to him.

"Thought you were gonna fuck me, Carter? What was it you said about how many orgasms you could give me before you do? I don't see me coming from sucking your cock."

He pulls me up from the back of my head, and my arms drop forward, resting over his. There's a predatory, pissed off look in his eye, and he brings me so far toward him that our lips are almost touching. "Enough of your mouth," he growls, releasing my hair and grabbing me.

With one hand, he knocks our glasses off the table onto the chair. One falls off and smashes on the ground, and I gasp when he flips me over onto the table and spanks my ass. I arch my back, the front of my dress removing the chill from the table.

My arms hit the hard surface in front of me, and foil tears behind me. I've barely had time to take a breath than Carter's hands are on my ass, spreading it, and his cock is roughly pushing its way into my pussy.

It hurts but it doesn't, and I cry out, resulting in a slap to my other ass cheek.

Fuck me, I love a spanker.

I moan again. Deliberately.

This time, though, he doesn't spank me. Once again, he winds my hair around his hand and tugs. It's harsher than before, and I'm all but looking at the ceiling. My back is totally curved, and he slams himself into me in a show of pure strength that hits all my right buttons. I get his point, to make me shut up, but all it does is drive another pleasured moan from my lips.

I lift my hips and push back into him so his cock gets deeper and his thrusts get longer, and fuck, fuck, fuck, fuck. His cock is so long and hard, his thrusts so powerful. His ability to fuck me until I lose my breath is unreal.

I can't breathe. Not right now. All I can do is ridiculous little sharp bursts of air that I doubt even make it to my lungs. He's there right behind me. He's driving into me relentlessly. My heart is thundering louder than before and my lungs are burning and my bloodstream is full of nothing but endorphins and pleasure and adrenaline and promises of a blinding orgasm that has the potential to knock me out.

"Not so sassy now, huh, Bee?" Raspy and broken, he speaks. "Not so fucking sassy now my cock is buried deep in your sweet pussy and you're at its mercy."

Another spank, and lust swamps me in a swath of heat.

Carter slaps his hands down onto the table either side of my body and continues his domination, thrusting harder and harder until my eyes water and I really can't breathe because there's nothing but pleasure, and stars, and blackness, and pleasure all over again.

I tremble everywhere. My stomach clenches. My legs are tight. My fingers are curled so far into my palms that my fists must be iron-like. It's bolt after bolt of desire and lust and everything else that goes into the making of an orgasm.

And, yeah. My scalp is stinging from his grip and my back aches from its permanent arch, but his cock pounding into me and his balls swinging and slapping against my clit has me edging closer and closer.

I hold my breath.

There.

The edge.

He stands.

Reaches round.

Presses his thumb.

To my clit.

I explode.

I scream.

He moves faster.

It's quick.

Harsh.

Rough.

Brutal.

Everything.

He releases my hair and I relax, collapsing onto the table. He leans forward, his chest against my back. Fucking hell. Fuck, shit, damn. There isn't an inch of me not feeling the waves of heat and trembles of oblivion he just gave me.

He slides his hands down my arms and lifts his head to undo his tie. I flex my wrists the second they're free and bend my arms to dive my fingers into my hair.

Jesus fucking Christ.

I have no words that don't start with 'fuck.'

Carter stands and with his hands planted on my ass once again, pulls out of me. He hooks his finger through my thong and repositions it over my pussy.

What a gentleman.

"It's a shame one night is all the time I have to offer a woman," he muses, pulling me up and spinning me into him. His arms wrap my body tightly, and I muster all my remaining strength so I don't fall into him. "Because you're a fucking delight, Bee."

"A delight. That's exactly what every woman wants to be called after sex," I breathe, my blood still thundering through my body almost deafeningly.

He smirks, the amusement in it reaching his eyes. He cups my chin and lifts my face, looking into my eyes. "I'd fuck you all night long if I could, baby. But I have business to attend to. There'll be a car waiting for you to take you home. Take the door to your left instead of going through the restaurant." He presses his lips against my cheek in a touch that feels warm but lacks any real heat, then releases me.

I grab the table to steady myself and watch as he does up his pants, rebuttons his shirt, replaces his tie and jacket, and walks out of the booth without another word, perfectly composed.

And even though I still have aftershocks shuddering through me, I straighten. I pull my dress down to cover my ass and grab my purse from the floor. Digging it in, I pull out twenty bucks, throw it on the table, then walk out of the booth myself.

There's a car waiting indeed. I doubt my twenty dollars even touched the price of the wine, but I can pay my way.

I pass the doorman, step outside the restaurant, flag a cab, and climb in.

And that's how you do a blind date—the blind isn't in not knowing who you're meeting.

It's in fucking them and knowing you'll never see them again.

CHAPTERTHREE

I hate Mondays.

My heels click against the linoleum floor of my office and echo around the spacious room. Mind you, it would be much more spacious if I didn't have whiteboards and corkboards and fabric swatches all over the place.

Hey—I never said it was fucking tidy.

I don't do tidy. I do organized chaos. I know where everything is, because it has its place—even if that place is the last spot you'd expect to find it. Like... a pile of color charts stuffed into the vase on my windowsill, or the flowers meant for that vase now dead and dry, resting on top of a pile of books about various middle-Eastern methods of organizing your house and the like.

I'm not sure I've ever read them, but whatever. It is what it is.

I sit at my desk and move a file from it so I can put my laptop down. A few more things shift, and it briefly crosses my mind that maybe I should tidy it...

Nah. Thought came and went before I could finish it.

I click on the Gmail shortcut on my desktop and flick open my diary. My morning is clear, so I do what I do best. I open a new tab on the browser and head straight for the Victoria's Secret website.

What? I got a coupon in the mail this morning and I didn't have time to look before I came here. I'm simply being a responsible adult and saving money. You know... When I should be earning it.

Good thing I work with my mom.

"Come in," I say when two sharp knocks echo through my office.

The door squeaks open, and my mom steps in. Her softly curled mahogany hair bounces off her shoulders as her heels click against the linoleum. With her hands on her hips, she peruses my less-than-tidy office with her blood red lips pursed tightly. "You really need to tidy this space."

"I know, I know." I shoot her my sweetest smile. "What's up?"

"Carlos double booked me," she says, absently collecting sheets together from one of my armchairs.

"Again?"

"Hmmm." Her dark eyes cut to me, and one of her perfectly shaped eyebrows quirks up in displeasure. "I think he was supposed to book this consultation with you, given your empty schedule this morning."

"Mrs. Cortez cancelled again. Something about having to get her bunions removed." Having an empty morning is a rarity, and she knows it. We didn't build this interior design company overnight. While I worked my ass off in college for my degree, Mom was working to build a clientele with one of the most prestigious interior design firms in New York City.

The day Donnelly Designs Inc. became a registered company with the state of New York, she brought the clientele with her—and with the clientele came rave reviews and solid recommendations.

This is the first empty morning I've had in weeks.

Mom tuts and puts a book back on my bookshelf. With her slim figure and almost wrinkleless skin, you wouldn't believe she's fifty. Of course, I'm certain her skin has had a little help from Botox, but she'll never admit to it. Unfortunately for me and my theories, she has Grandpa on her side insisting that Nanna was the same.

"Sienna Cortez has more bunions than anyone I've ever met in my life. If she does it for a fourth time, you politely tell her that she'll have to find another designer to... What does she want doing now?"

"Her kitchen."

"Tell her to hire a builder." Mom sniffs and turns. "Anyway, as I was saying, Carlos double booked me. Since one of my appointments is a home visit with Louis, I need you to take over the other."

"Sure." I reach for a notepad and eventually find one in my desk drawer. And a pen… Ho hum.

Mom rolls her eyes and hands me a pen from a pot on my windowsill.

Aha. That's where I put the fuckers.

"Thanks. So, where do you need me to go?" I ask, looking up, pen poised and ready to write down the address.

"A restaurant on 58ᵗʰ street." She wipes a fingertip across one of my shelves, and I barely hold back my own eye-roll when she wrinkles her face up and wipes the dust from her finger. She focuses her dark eyes on me, then glances pointedly at my notepad. "Two eighty E, 58ᵗʰ street. Carter's."

I freeze, horror washing over me in a chilling shiver. "Wh-where?"

"Good Lord, Bee, don't make me repeat myself." She sighs. "I've called ahead and said you're going. The owner, Carter Hughes, will be waiting for you at eleven a.m. You have plenty of time to wipe a wet cloth over your shelves and perhaps have Carlos order you some form of filing system. Then again, he'd probably purchase you a dressing table instead."

Carter Hughes. A consultation.

Right.

Because we didn't have enough of a consultation not forty-eight hours ago.

"Bee?" Mom says my name for what I'm assuming isn't the first time. "Can you do it?"

"I…" Damn you and your bunions, Mrs. Cortez. "Sure, Mom."

"Excellent." She claps her hands together, and for the first time she entered my office, her face breaks into a wide smile. "I'm lead to believe that he's meeting with several companies throughout the day, including Parker Interiors." Her smile drops and her lip curls in disgust.

Ah. That'll be her old employer who tried to sue her when she left, taking half their client portfolio with her.

Excellent. So this consultation is personal. In more fucking ways than I'd like it to be.

"Make sure we get this contract," Mom orders me, stalking back toward my door. "I'm counting on you for this, Bee. Carter Hughes is incredibly influential and if he hires us and is happy with us, it opens even more doors for us." The door clicks shut with an echo that's all too final.

Believe me, Mom. I know exactly how influential Carter Hughes is—he's also real convincing. After it, it took him all of ten minutes to get his hand inside my panties.

I shudder at the memory. God, what are the chances? I'm certain Karma is royally fucking with me right now. I'm not sure what I did to the temperamental little bitchtit, but maybe it's as simple as she thinks it's about time I came face to face with one of my conquests.

The barista at Starbucks doesn't count. I mean, I totally knew he worked there when I slipped him my card. He had just handed me a caramel hot chocolate, after all. I just didn't expect him to call me.

I sigh and rest my cheek on my hand. I probably should have guessed that my carefree personal life would catch up to my professional one in the end. Just, for the love of fucking God, why does it have to be with Carter Hughes?

Damn it. Damn it all to hell and back again.

This truly is karma at her finest. I can still feel the sweet burn of pleasure from his skillful touch. I can still remember the way he played my body as though I were a piano.

I think I'm still having the goddamn orgasm.

Seeing him is not going to work out.

Shit.

I wring my sweaty hands together as I sit in the back of the cab.

This is such a bad idea. Me going to this restaurant and seeing this man is exactly what nightmares are made of. What was I going to tell Mom though? Let's be real. I could hardly tell her that I couldn't complete this consultation because I screwed the man on Saturday night.

Shit. Charley's gonna have a fucking field day with this.

"Ma'am? We're here," my cab driver says.

I take a deep breath and hand him the fare before stepping out on the New York sidewalk. The sun is glimmering its way through the skyscrapers, its warmth unbothered by the tall, glass buildings in its way. I revel in the sensation on the sunshine on my skin and turn my face into it.

For a moment, I can pretend I'm not here. I imagine I'm on a beach in the Bahamas, sipping on a fruity cocktail. I'm stepping out onto the balcony of my hotel in the Jamaican morning sun. I'm dancing in the afternoon Mexican heat.

The illusions are broken by the tooting of horns and distant whirr of a siren.

Ugh. New York can't even give me two minutes, can it?

My stomach coils in apprehension as I study the outside of the restaurant. With its clean lines and black mirrored walls that are broken by perfectly polished windows, not to mention the thick, block letters proclaiming it to be Carter's, it's a wonder I never noticed its striking look at the weekend.

Then again, I never have paid much attention to my surroundings. Ironic, considering my job. Or perhaps it's because of.

Who knows?

Not to mention that this place apparently has two doors in, because this is the door I came out of.I glance at the dainty watch circling my wrist. Five to eleven. I should really make my presence known or risk being fired from the company I own thirty-three percent of.

Mom would too, just to teach me a lesson.

I approach the heavy wooden black door just to the left of the restaurant, per the email instructions Carlos finally emailed to me five minutes ago. Apparently the man has never mastered the art of preparation and his organizational skills resemble a toddler's far more than mine ever could.

With a deep breath filling my lungs to the brim with oxygen, I clasp the thick sample book to my chest and rap my knuckles against the door. Two seconds later, I notice the bell, black too, and press it.

More horns beep as the traffic merges at the end of the block.

Slowly, the door opens. A young woman who can be no older than my own twenty-six years fills the space in front of me. Her blouse is perfectly pressed and well fitted, and her black pencil skirt leads down to skyscraper heels. Blue eyes peruse me as slick blonde bangs graze her eyebrows. "Can I help you?"

24

I force a smile. "My name is Bee Donnelly. I'm here on behalf of Donnelly Designs."

Blondie purses her lips and grasps an iPad seemingly out of nowhere. "We have a Carla Donnelly on the schedule."

"My mother," I confirm. "Something came up for her. She said she'd called ahead and informed you I'd be coming."

She rolls her eyes and sets the iPad down. Who the fuck knows where? Seems like any area behind her is made solely of darkness and possibly bitch-pill-fed demons. She produces an iPhone from the same blackness and scrolls. "Oh yes. I have a missed call from her. Two seconds please."

I take a deep, calming breath as she turns away, the phone to her ear.

"For fuck sake, Joanna. Let her in. She's hardly a terrorist."

I'd know that voice anywhere.

Mostly because the last words I heard it say were that I'm a 'fucking delight.'

"Sir, I'm simply confir—"

"Joanna. Escort her into the bar. Thank you." A shadowy figure strolls behind her.

Blondie—apparently named Joanna, although I will assume her parents missed a damn good trick on the Barbie front—looks to the ceiling. Her cheeks flush as she takes a step back and opens the door wider. "My apologies, Ms. Donnelly. Please come in and forgive my rudeness."

I wave it off. "Don't worry, honey. I have a demon-boss of my own."

Her lips twitch. "Your mother."

"Sssh." I touch my finger to my lips. "Don't say the word. You may just summon her."

She glances down, fighting a smile, then sweeps her arm elegantly. "Follow me. Mr. Hughes is waiting for you."

Yes. He sure does have that habit of waiting… Once you're at his mercy, that is.

Holy fuck, Bee. This is not the kind of thought you need to be having right now. You're here to design his—wait. No. I'm not here to design a thing. I already designed the man an orgasm for the love of fucking God.

The contract though.

Right. The contract.

Focus, Bee.

Sweet fuck. How can I? This wasn't in my plan. Nowhere near it. Neither was the blind date, so really, this is Charley's fault. The bitch.

"Take a seat," Joanna offers, motioning to a black bar stool. "He'll be right with you."

"Thank you." I set the giant portfolio down on the black glass bar. Another fact I missed this weekend. Holy hell, was I truly that wrapped up in Carter Hughes that I didn't notice a thing about this... bar? Restaurant? Whatever it is he's running here?

Yes. I was. Because I'm a slut and I'm proud of that.

And there's a sentence I never thought I'd have to say to myself.

Judge me all you like. We all have an inner whore inside us.

Charlie Hunnam. Ryan Reynolds. Adam Levine. Julian Edelman. Jamie Dornan. Brad Pitt. Channing Tatum. Ian Somerhalder. Cristiano Ronaldo. Matt Bomer. Joe Manganiello.

If you can think of them and have dry panties, then you're clearly an alien who has no place on this world.

I close my eyes briefly to center myself. Work. Consult. Give opinion. Be a real woman. Don't be a puddle. I'm here to work and I need to remember that.

New York City might be crazy, but it isn't that big. I should have guessed as soon as he told me he owned the restaurant that I'd see him again. You know. If I'd have paid attention to the restaurant in the first place.

Fuckity fucky fucker fuckit.

What is wrong with me?

A lot. Apparently a whole lot of stuff is wrong with me.

Goddamn it. I can't be this flustered for this meeting. It's like offering myself up as prey for him. If I continue to act like a teenager in the throes of her first crush I may as well just bunch up my skirt, sit my fine ass on this bar and just let him have his way with me.

Shit. That doesn't help either.

Dammit. Why am I such a slut?

From right now, this very second, I swear that the next time I allow a man between my legs is if he's either a doctor or my husband.

Okay. Husband is drastic. Way drastic. Who knows how long it'll take me to find the one?

Still, it's time for a battery-operated boyfriend. At least I know the next time I run into him I won't have to make conversation—and there's no chance of him coming before me. As long as you keep an eye on the battery level, of course.

All righty then. Deep breath, Bee. Let's focus on the fact that the kind of escapade you just had with Carter Hughes is a thing of the past. What an esca—

No.

I touch my fingertips to the portfolio and take a deep breath. The sound of a throat cleaning has me looking up at the figure half-standing in the shadows. His dark hair is as slick and smoothly styled as I remember it. His suit is crisp and well-fitting, the fabric stretching easily over his shoulders without straining. It reeks of expense and of class, but I ignore that tiny fact as I lift my gaze to his face.

His jaw, sharp and angular and dusted with dark, perfectly trimmed stubble, is tight. Pink lips set in the tempting spread of facial hair are quirked to one side in a knowing smirk, and heat pools in my stomach as I remember exactly what those lips can do.

But as always, it's his eyes. His emerald green eyes are dazzling, invasive in their scrutiny as they trawl across my face and my body, from the gentle curls of my dark hair and down to my Louboutin-clad feet.

He's as hot as ever.

I need a handyman. I'm screwed.

"Ms. Donnelly." Carter approaches me with one hand stretched out. I slide off the stool and hold my own out. He clasps it firmly, his fingers wrapping around mine. The grip is steady, the sizzle of his skin hot against mine. He pulls me into him, and with one hand resting against my side, he whispers, "So good to see you again."

So we're playing this game. "Mr. Hughes," I reply, my voice leaning to the seductive side. I pull back and take my hand from his. "How are you?"

His eyes flash with the recognition that just hit me. "Very well. Yourself?"

"Couldn't be better, thank you."

He waves toward the stool I just vacated, and I lean back, retaking my seat. He sits on the one next to me. "Shall we get started?" He reaches one strong hand up and adjusts his tie.

Oh boy.

I fight the squirm that tickles through my lower body and respond with a smile. "Absolutely." I adjust my skirt so I can cross one leg over the over. His eyes drop to my legs as I smooth my skirt back out. "Tell me more about what you have in mind."

The slow, purposeful lift of his gaze burns through me. Damn, those eyes. They're intense and calculating, but not in a cold way. They see right through me. He knows I've seen his game and raised him. I get the feeling I won't be the only one lifting the stakes.

He leans against the bar and rests his forearm against it. His fingers tap against the glass surface one by one, making no more than a quiet tap. "Joanna?" he calls, his eyes still focused on me. "Could you get me and Ms. Donnelly a cup of coffee?"

"Of course," she says from somewhere behind me.

"And hold my calls." He tilts his head to the side, his lips twitching. "I don't want to be disturbed."

My eyebrows shoot up at the sound of a door closing. A shiver also dances down my spine, but I'm not going to focus on that. I'm going to focus on the assumption that I want coffee and he doesn't want to be disturbed.

"Presumptuous," I remark, removing a notepad and pen from my purse.

"Which part?"

"Both."

"Depends how you take it." His smile simply grows.

I look to the ceiling and inhale sharply. Resolutely, I place my notepad and pen on the bar and meet Carter's gaze. "Mr. Hughes, I'm here on behalf of my mother and our company. Whether you arranged this consultation before or after our previous meeting isn't something I, quite frankly, give a shit about. What I do care about is coming here, doing my job, and going away to design something that will give Donnelly Designs a chance to be hired by you. I would appreciate that whatever happened in the past stay there."

"Your company?" he asks, still not dropping the smirk. "You own it?"

Not seeing what this has to do with anything, but whatever. "Partially. It's the brainchild of us both. I have the minority, but one day I'll own it all, so…" I shrug one shoulder. "It's important to me that we have a good, honest portfolio."

"Are you suggesting that I'd hire you simply because I enjoy the way your mouth feels when it's around my cock?"

I choke on my own saliva. "I can't say that's the way I'd have worded it."

"In my experience, you're a straight to the point woman, Bee Donnelly. Answer the question."

Fine. "Yes."

"See?" He leans forward, his eyes sparkling with amusement. "Wasn't too hard, was it?"

I glance at his pants. "Nope."

The action stills him. "I booked this before we met," he says in a low voice. "I assumed it were merely coincidence that you had the same surname. Donnelly isn't exactly unique or rare."

If I didn't want to know where he was going, I'd be offended.

"But to address your inaccurate opinion, I don't hire people based on how well they fuck. If I did, we'd be having a very different type of consultation." His jaw tics as heat floods my cheeks. "Let's move through to the restaurant and we can talk."

He gets up and turns away. My heart is twisting in both annoyance and embarrassment. I grab my things and follow him.

Sorry, Mom. I both fucked and offended a prospective client. My bad.

God she's gonna kill me. And she's gonna make it painful.

Carter leads me through the bar and opens the door to the restaurant. I take a succession of slow, deep breaths as we step out into the bar, and I won't lie, I'm thankful to leave that part. I know that on the other side of the room is the booths.

A place I really, really hope he doesn't want redesigning.

I adjust the waistband of my skirt and take a step up next to him.

"The restaurant." He runs his finger along the leaf of a bushy indoor plant. "I want it redesigned more in line with the bar."

"The style and scheme?" I question, my mouth going dry. I hope he doesn't mean the… environment. Can you imagine digging into your salmon or steak to the sound of a sexual rendezvous?

He cuts his eyes to me, and his lips do that twitchy thing again. "Yes, the style and color scheme. The bar is a… newer addition to the space. It was part of my former living space. When I moved out, I decided to convert it and the upper floor."

"What's in the upper floor?" I swallow. The way this place is going, it's probably whips, chains, and shackles.

As if he can read my mind, Carter turns his whole body toward me and meets my eyes. "Joanna's apartment."

Ah.

"Don't worry yourself, Ms. Donnelly. I don't have a secret sex lair where I whisk young, hot women away to. Unless, of course, they ask."

"You just have a semi-public sex bar?" I lift an eyebrow, setting my purse on a table.

"I told you before—I have a very elite clientele with specific tastes. Some people relish knowing they're fucking with other people walking past."

"Is that really all it's used for?"

"Of course not. Sometimes people book them for private dates, business meetings, or simply time alone. But, I'd suppose… Ninety percent of the time they're booked for solely sexual purposes."

Okay. I know I did it, but it sounds really peculiar when you put it like that. Booths that are booked for sexual purposes in an apparently upscale restaurant in the middle of New York City. It's very… Well. Odd, isn't it?

"You look confused."

"I'm fine." I draw myself out of my thoughts and focus on the portfolio. I flip it open to the section full of my previous restaurants and some of Mom's. "Take a look through these and make a note of any you like and what you like so I can incorporate those elements into my final design. Do you have a blueprint of the building?"

"Yes…" he says the word slowly, as if he's testing it out by rolling it around his tongue.

So I changed the subject with a whiplash-inducing speed. I can't think about those goddamn booths anymore or I'm gonna need to go change my panties before I head back to the office.

"Perfect. Do you have it to hand?"

"Let me find Joanna and bring the coffee. I'll ask her to get it ready for you."

"Thank you." I flash him a smile that's more confident than I feel and pull my camera from my bag. Carter sweeps past me, his long stride having him through the door in seconds.

Only now, with him gone, do I feel like I can breathe properly. Only now can my heart slow and my hands stop trembling.

I focus on the space around me. You can tell it hasn't been painted for a couple years, never mind fully refitted. Not that you can tell—hell, I definitely didn't notice on Saturday because I didn't give a crap—but still… bringing this up to the quality of the bar area will be a bit of a job.

Still, I'm up to this.

I walk around the restaurant and snap pictures of everything. Although the blueprints will show me where everything is, having the pictures means I'll be able to draw in the majority of the tables where they sit currently.

Ugh, why are they all square or rectangular?

Note to self: make circular tables a necessity.

No reason other than the fact that I like them. And isn't it so nice to be able to see everyone you're having dinner with if you're in a big group?

When I'm done with the pictures, I spin find Carter flicking through the portfolio. He's lost his jacket, and the sleeves of his white shirt are rolled up to just above his elbows, highlighting his toned biceps perfectly. "See anything you like?"

His gaze finds mine, then slowly, oh so slowly, he peruses my body once more, only speaking when our eyes meet again. "Plenty."

"Ooookay," I breathe. "I'm going through to the bar to take photos for style references." I walk away just as quickly as I turned, noticing the coffee on the table at the last moment.

Ah, damn it. Oh well. I'll just stop in Starbucks.

The bar area is dimly lit from the small windows above the booths and from the main door, so I reach for the light switch and flip it. The area fills with light, and for the first time, it hits me just how big this space is… And how very different it looks in the daytime compared to the evening.

The curtains to the booths are open and secured at the sides, and each booth could easily sit six to eight people. The seats are wider than I'd expected. I guess they look bigger than they feel, even when you're lying on your back with room to spare.

Unlike the bar, the circular tables in the center of each look like they're made of wood. Solid black wood with a shiny lacquered surface on top, but still wood.

I guess you don't want people smashing tables if they get vigorous.

I swallow and snap a few pictures. The bar in the restaurant is easily redesigned to match this, but probably not black. Charcoal, maybe, to soften. Black, white, and gray. I run my finger along the edge of the bar, careful not to leave any fingerprints on the perfectly polished surface. I can see Carter's from where he touched it earlier.

Really, this bar is amazing. Small and intimate, yet he's right. Anyone could, in theory, walk past and know exactly what you're doing in one of them.

And it is. A thrill. To know that.

My clit aches at the memory, a dull sensation that comes to life when I reach the booth we were in. Every booth is identical, not a single thing differing them, but I know this was it, because it's furthest away from the restaurant.

My eyes flutter shut, and I steel myself as I hear the door go. I glance to the side, and shiny black shoes move across the floor, attached to legs with perfectly pressed black pants covering them. I'm not a fool. I know it's Carter.

"Is there anything in particular you'd like brought through?" I ask, my voice cracking halfway through.

"The design concept," he answers, still walking toward me. "The general style, color scheme, the ambiance. I've noted the work you've done previously and pulled the things I like. I doubt it'll be too hard for you to come up with an impressive design."

"How long do I have?" My tongue darts across my lips.

"Three days."

"Three days?" I spin to face him. "Are you serious? I have to find and source all of the things I need then put them together in a comprehensive design in *three days?*"

His green eyes seem brighter as they dart to the booth then back to me. My skin tingles at his silent innuendo, and my heart thumps erratically against my ribs. "Or don't," he murmurs, stepping closer to me. The low huskiness of his voice wrap around me and bathe me in lust-filled warmth. "I won't deny it, Bee. I don't want to hire you. I don't want you in this building where I'll be forced to see you every single day."

"Then don't." I step back, but he only mirrors my action, coming toward me once more.

Carter closes his fingertips around my upper arm, holding me in place gently. "I will not hire someone because of a personal history, but I also refuse to not hire someone. If your design is best, I'll hire Donnelly Designs. If not, I won't. It's that simple."

"If you don't want me here, I'd rather you not hire me. Full stop." I tug my arm away from him.

In one sleek, expert move, Carter Hughes pins me against his bar. He wrenches my camera from my grasp and sets it on the glass surface behind me, then grabs the edge of the bar, trapping me. His hard body is hot, and his pelvis is pinning me in place.

It's not all that's pinning me in place.

"I don't want you here because I don't like you," he whispers, his hot breath fanning across my lips. "I don't want you here, because I want to fuck you." He takes hold of my hand and presses his thumb to my wrist, satisfaction hitting his gaze when he feels my raging pulse. "I want to take you take you into one of those booths and bend you over the table. I want to hoist you onto this bar and bury myself inside you. I want to push you against the wall and fuck you until you pass out from your pleasure."

Oh Jesus. This escalated quickly. Real fucking quickly.

I can't breathe. At all. I'm on fire everywhere—from my lungs burning as they fight for oxygen, from the red-hot desire my heart is pounding through my body with my blood, and from the ridiculous heat trickling its way over my skin until it collects and centers in my clit.

"I don't want you here because I'm certain that if you are, I'll fulfill every single one of those desires, and quickly," he murmurs, his mouth now barely a breath away from mine. "And that would not be good for anyone, would it?"

I lean back as far as I can and let out a shuddery breath. "If you hire me, I'll be here to work, not play. So trust me when I say it will remain entirely profess —"

"Like right now?" he asks, a knowing smile playing with his lips. "Like how professional this is, with you pinned against the bar and my cock pressing against you? You can't even look at the damn booth, Bee. I watched you. I watched your pretty little cheeks flush as you glanced inside it and remembered how hard you came. How many times you came. So don't stand here and tell me it'll remain professional, because we both know that if I decide I'm going to fuck you, I'm going to fuck you."

An indignant streak shoots down my spine, and I straighten. Yes, my mouth is right by his. Yes, our breath is mingling. I'm afraid that if I lick my lips, I'll accidentally lick his. My breasts are heaving and brushing against his chest, my white blouse a perfect match to his shirt.

Carter reaches up and twines a fistful of my hair around his fingers. The action only brings us even closer together. "Don't pretend you won't give in." His lips brush mine with every word, but the touch is the furthest thing from a kiss. "You're falling apart right now and I've barely touched you."

I wish he didn't have to be right.

"This is highly inappropriate," I whisper, resisting the urge to grab his shirt and wrap my legs around him and climb him like a tree.

"Yet you haven't pushed me away."

"Yeah, well, you're stronger than me," I say lamely.

He laughs. God, the rich, decadent sound flows over me, and just when he leans in, he pauses. The breath that sings his hesitation passes through my parted lips and dances across the tip of my tongue. I inhale, breathing him in, expecting, waiting, for the touch.

It doesn't come.

All that comes is a light laugh, and the cluck of resignation as he pushes away. He shakes his head. His shoulders are tight as he walks away and into the restaurant.

Do I follow?

Do I stand here?

You know what? I'm gonna stand here. Because my whole body is freakin' trembling and I don't think I can move anyway.

Jesus. Fuck. Christ. Asshole. I don't think this will work at all.

Carter storms back through the door, my purse in one hand and the portfolio in the other. "Your notepad with my requests are inside your purse." He hands them to me, and I hook the purse over my arm, then tuck the portfolio against my chest. His fingers burn through the fabric of my blouse as he touches my back and guides me toward the door. With his hand clutching the doorknob, he turns to me, barely inching the door opens. "Fuck, Bee," he hisses out, stepping back and rubbing his hand through his hair. It messes up the usually perfectly styled locks, and I have to fight my smile. "Please do a really bad job in your design. I might just go crazy if you're around all day."

One of my eyebrows quirks upward. Do a bad job? Is he kidding me? I don't want this contract any more than he wants to give me it, but I'm not going to flunk it the way I flunked Geography in high school.

For the record, Milwaukee is *not a* cocktail.

I brush his hand from the doorknob then grasp it with my own. The door is weighty, but I pull it open with one tug and take a step out onto the bustling, sunny sidewalk, and then turn. Our eyes meet as the sun warms my skin. "Oh... Carter. Don't hope I'll do a bad job... You need to hope someone else does better."

CHAPTERFOUR

"*I*'m going to *kill* you."

Charley rolls her eyes. "Oh, please. I made you go on a date—not take a ride on his disco stick."

A small noise like a strangled scream escapes me. "I hate myself."

"No you don't. You just hate your inner slut."

"No, no. I like her. She stops me being too uptight. I just hate that outside Bee doesn't argue with her."

My best friend picks up a canvas picture of a flower. "I suppose. You do need your inner slut when you work with your mom. Especially your mom. No offence," she adds quickly, putting the canvas back on the shelf and glancing at me. "I love her, but damn."

"No kidding," I mutter, finding a gorgeous black-framed photo of the New York skyline. I take a picture of it with my phone and note down the price.

Mom just about lost her shit when I finally got back to the office. So what if I took a detour to Starbucks, to book a manicure, and had my cab driver drive around a couple of blocks a few times? I needed to breathe. I needed to take every bit of Carter Hughes' essence left inside me and let it go before going back and talking about him again.

Needless to say, after thirty minutes of grilling about the meeting, another thirty with her asking me why my office still looks like a tornado traveled through it with whiplash, and two hours of her flitting between clients and asking poor Carlos for everything but his first born and testicles.

Mom's difficult, for sure. But she means well in all she does... Even if she does those things in a way that errs on the side of mean.

"She doesn't know, does she?" Charley asks, pointing to a clear glass vase filled with shiny black stones. Black and white fake flowers are sprouting from the top, and I snap a picture, if only so she doesn't get offended. I'm dying to get hold of her apartment and take her shopping. "Earth to Bee."

"Know what?" I ask, feigning innocence.

"That you made like a football in the end zone and scored with your prospective client."

I roll my eyes. Sheesh. Can no one say 'had sex with' these days? "No, my mother does *not* know, and neither will she find out."

I can't imagine the hell that will rain down upon me if she ever found out. It's actually terrifying to consider it.

"You can't really think that."

I run my hand over the back of a leather bucket chair. Charley gives me a thumbs up. "I do, okay? She can't find out. She'd probably force me to sell my share of the business to her and write me out of her will. It doesn't matter if I get the contract or not. If she finds out, she's going to think that if I get it, it'll be because we… you know."

"Horizontal tangoed."

"Yeah. That. And if I don't get it, she'll think it'll be because we… well."

"Did the wall-waltz."

"Oh my God. Just say sex!" I snap, finding black leather dining chairs that match the bucket chairs. They come in charcoal too, so I add those to my list of potential items for the restaurant.

"Fine. You sexed each other so hard you can't even be in the same room," Charley summarizes, picking up one of the black mats on the table. "Accurate?"

"I… yeah. Shut up."

"And now you're going to design the shit out of his restaurant and hope that someone else does it better."

"I… yeah."

"Why? Why not just screw it up deliberately or do such a basic design that there'll be no way he can pick you?"

"Because..." I sigh, turning to face her. "I don't want to do that. It's not honest. I don't want to work for him, but I don't want someone to see bad designs and think they could be my best work. Plus Mom will know. She knows I don't half-ass anything, even if I only have three days to do it."

Charlie blows out a long breath and pauses. Her eyes cut to me, but she averts her gaze as she picks up a candle holder then puts it back down again.

"What?"

"This could be the most obvious question ever," she hedges, "But why not just refuse on the basis that the time frame is too short? The other designers will have had more notice than you. Why did you only get three days?"

"Scheduling? I don't know. It was Mom's appointment, remember."

"Was it?"

"Charley, he said so. I don't think Carter Hughes has to stoop that low just to see a woman again. He didn't even look like he particularly wanted me there." Well, he wanted me there. He made that very clear—just not in the way I should have been there.

"Just sleep with him again. Get it over and done with then refuse on the basis of your irresistible personal relationship."

"Irresistible personal relationship? Really? You think I should walk up to a sexy as sin, rich as hell, successful man and tell him I can't work for him because he's irresistible, right after he's told me the numerous ways he wants me naked and against him?" My eyebrows shoot up. "Yeah, yeah, let's do that. Let's see how long that conversation lasts."

"Jesus. You're bitchy when you need sex."

"I'm bitchy all the time. I just like you enough to not voice it all the time."

"Oh, I'm honored." She snorts, but flashes me a grin anyway. "Do you have enough stuff here? I'm starving. Like my stomach is about to nibble its way through my gut hungry."

I roll my eyes. "Fine. Let's get food."

Sometimes having a best friend who's the ice to your fire isn't a good thing. Sure, she's generally more reserved and quieter than me and usually holds me back before I blow, but it also means that she thinks before she acts. I tend to act and then regret. As evidenced by this past weekend.

I barely slept a wink last night after considering her idea about the appointment.

Did he actually book it before we met? Mom never said if it was a late booking or not. Then again, she was more concerned with my office than anything else. But she did also call ahead… Someone had to have gotten that message and passed it on to him, right?

The more I think about it, the more certain I am that Carter Hughes absolutely knew I'd be the one coming. I also believe he's the kind of man who hires companies and staff personally. For all his 'it's not my business what happens in these booths' bullshit on Saturday night was likely just that. Bullshit.

I'd bet anything that he researched Donnelly Designs before he booked the consultation. I bet he knew exactly who I was the second we were introduced on Saturday evening.

I bet he didn't care a single bit, because the appointment wasn't with me.

What if it was? What if he'd been booked with me? Then what would have happened? I couldn't have walked out of dinner… But I sure as hell wouldn't have slept with him.

Although… What if I'd thought to ask Charley who my date was? Or looked at the name of the restaurant?

What if is always the issue, isn't it? What could you change? I'd change just about fucking everything in this situation if I could. I wish I could. I wish I could take all of this and erase every moment.

I click my mouse as I work on the digital bones of what will be my design for the restaurant.

Either way, he knew who I was when we had that date. I'm sure of it.

How dare he? How dare he do what he did knowing there was a possibility that he could work with Donnelly Designs? *How fucking dare he?*

Maybe Charley was right. Maybe refusing to do this is for the best. But then what would be the point in that? I'd just have to explain my reasoning to my mother and get my ass kicked… And then he'd win, wouldn't he?

Not in the sense that this is a game. This is business, and despite the fact you have to bend the rules of business to come out on top, I'm willing to fight.

If my design is his favorite and he hires me, he couldn't touch me. You don't mix work and pleasure. You don't play while you conduct business. If that were the case, you'd have a bottle of vodka next to a fucking chess board on your desk, wouldn't you?

No. I can resist Carter Hughes. I know that much. After all, wasn't he the one who approached me yesterday? Wasn't he the one who crossed the line between talking and flirting, then continued to undress me with his eyes?

Wasn't he the one who put into words all the things he'd like to do to me?

God. It was so much easier in high school when boys just jerked off in the shower to those fantasies. It's such a bastard when boys become men and have no qualms about telling you how and where they'd like to fuck you.

It's hot. Don't get me wrong. I needed a new pair of panties stat.

But it's still a bastard.

Because now I'm thinking of those things, aren't I? I don't just have the memories of the weekend, of the way I squirmed against his wicked tongue, or the way he pushed me to oblivion more times than anyone ever had before. No. No fucking siree. Now I'm imagining the asshole with me against the wall while his tongue explores me. Now I'm imagining him setting me on the bar, opening my legs, and driving into me until nothing makes sense anymore.

Now I'm thinking that I really can't resist him.

And to think. The man has never kissed me. Not even once.

Oddly enough it makes total sense. Kisses are intimate things. More intimate than sex, in a way. With kisses, it's the overwhelming sensation of being taken to another place without your feet ever leaving the ground. It's the slow build of desire that can only hum with life and electricity when lips meet. It's the feverish way each kiss becomes hotter than the last until reason becomes too much to comprehend and you're driven by nothing but instinct.

Yes. Kisses are absolutely the most intimate thing in this world.

And I would very much like to protect my mouth from Carter Hughes.

Perhaps I'll get a human muzzle.

For him, that is. Then maybe he won't be able to tell me any of the things he wants to do.

Although… that might be illegal. Ho hum.

I grab a Post-It and click my pen. *Check if it's legal to muzzle a human.* What? It's worth a search.

I put the pen down and push back from my desk. The wheels of my chair squeak as they roll, and I blink harshly several times, as though that movement will alleviate the ache growing behind my eyes. I've been staring at this computer for three hours without moving, and not only have my fingers seized up and my eyes gone blurry, my ass feels like it's been sat in ice for hours it's so numb.

It's almost impossible to concentrate with all this crap going on in my head. There's really only one way to find out, isn't there?

I sigh and pad through my office barefoot. My door opens silently, and I look out into the spacious waiting area. Design magazines and mini portfolios litter the glass coffee tables surrounded by plush blue sofas in the center of the floor, and Carlos' desk is directly opposite those.

He's on the phone right now, so I walk across the empty area and check the magazines. Carlos is supposed to check and update them every two weeks, but who knows if he's done it? He didn't last time and got his balls handed to him by Mom.

He hasn't done it again. I collect the outdated ones, roll them up, and put them in the titanium trash can just behind his counter. The phone clicks as he puts it back in the hold and he winces at me, somehow managing to blow his blonde hair from his face at the very same time.

"Sorry," he hurries out. "I was going to do it this afternoon."

"Just make sure you collect the new ones, okay? She still hasn't forgiven you for that double booking." Neither have I, I want to add. I don't, though. Carlos is also a bit of a gossip. "Talking of that double booking…" I lean forward and glimpse at the open diary right in front of him. "Carter Hughes—the appointment Mom gave me yesterday. When did he book?"

"Carter Hughes…" Carlos mutters, grabbing a notepad and flicking through it. "I'm pretty sure he called on Tuesday. Why?"

"Tight deadline," I explain. "I was curious why it was."

"You were both fully booked," he responds and puts the notepad back. "I didn't know Carla had an appointment with Louis because it wasn't in the diary."

My lips twitch to one side. "Carlos, if my mom's appointments with Louis are about his house, then I'm pretty sure the conversations are conducted between his bedsheets," I whisper. "The man's been getting his house redesigned for a year now."

"That's reasonable. It's a big house."

"Oh, sure. But who needs their dining room redecorating twice in that time?"

His response is a stare. "Point well made."

"Thank you." I tap my nails against the counter and spin on the balls of my feet. "Can you hold all my calls this afternoon? I have to get this design done for Carter Hughes. I already had to reschedule eight appointments because the man gave me a deadline tighter than a city full of virgin vaginas."

Carlos snorts. "All right. Any particular message?"

The previous one would do if I didn't have a professional image to uphold. "Just that I'm incredibly busy and to leave a message. I'll get back to everyone at the end of the week."

"No problem."

"Thanks." I smile and close my office door behind me. A stack of folders falls off my shelf, scattering sheets of paper across the floor. I groan and bend down to pick them up.

Maybe Mom has a point about my office.

CHAPTERFIVE

I stare at one completed design for *Carter's* spread across my desk.

I think I only slept like two hours last night, but it's done. And I'm not blowing glitter up my own ass here, but I'm pretty sure it's up there with my best ever designs. I don't know whether it's because I love the class of a monochrome theme or because I want to prove my point to him.

I wasn't lying when I told him to hope someone does a better job. I know my skills. I've worked for years to hone them to the standard I have them. I've bust my ass to reach this level and I'm not gonna half-ass something just because I fucked the guy.

Secretly, I think I worked harder on this. Ordinarily, I'd never take a project that gave me such little time to come up with a whole concept for such a large space. Sure, he was pretty certain on the kind of thing he wanted, but it's not easy.

I wanted to prove to Carter Hughes that I'm not intimidated by him or his sexy as fuck tactics. I'm not intimidated by the way he says dirty things in that low and husky voice of his.

If he thought he could scare me off with seduction, he thought wrong. He needs to spend a little bit less time in his fucking sex bar and reconnect with the real world, because I'm not seduced.

The shrill ring of my phone pierces the air, and I grab it. "Bee Donnelly."

"Carter Hughes is on the line for you," Carlos says.

"Put him through," I order, sitting up in my chair.

"Yes, ma'am."

The lines goes dead for a few seconds, then the husky voice that belongs to Carter Hughes rumbles down the line. "Ms. Donnelly," he says smoothly. "How are you today?"

"Fine, thank you. And yourself?"

"I'm very well. I assume you're done with your design proposal for my restaurant?"

"You assume correctly." I cross my feet at my ankles and lean forward on my desk, propping myself up with my elbows. "Although I'm pretty sure I never received instructions on how to get the design to you."

If smirks were audible, I think his would be screaming. "You'll have to bring it to me. I'm busy."

"I'll have to bring it to you?" My eyebrows shoot up. "I'm not your personal bitch, Mr. Hughes."

"No... But you are doing something that will get you a potential client."

"I rearranged six consultations with potential clients in the last three days because of your unreasonable demand. Believe me when I say I could have gained all six while I've been working on this for you."

"All the more reason to try and get my business, don't you think?" he asks dryly.

The man is infuriating. I'm almost certain that I'm getting to the point where I want to take the design to him, except I'll smack him around his handsome, smug face instead. "Here's an idea, Mr. Hughes. I have three appointments this afternoon that I can't reschedule. I'm going to see my appointments through and then I'll be working late to catch up on the things that fell by the wayside because of you. I'll be in my office until ten p.m. with your design. I'm sure, if you really want to see it, that you can find time to stop by and collect it."

"That isn't how this—"

A knock at my door makes me cut him off. "My next appointment is here. Ten p.m. Good afternoon, Mr. Hughes."

I hang up with an oddly triumphant feeling flowing through my body. God. Standing up to righteous assholes has always given me a sick pleasure. Knowing that he is the righteous asshole I just stood up to...

Well it puts the fucking zippidy in my goddamn doodaa, I'll tell you that.

"Bee?" Carlos knocks on my door once again. "Your two o'clock is here."

"Be right out," I reply, getting up and straightening my dress. I grab a stack of books from my client chair and put them on the bookshelf before opening the door.

Today feels like a good day.

It's been seven hours since my conversation with Carter Hughes and I haven't heard a fucking word from him.

Seems like the man can give it, but he can't take it.

I wonder how it makes him feel to know that there's a woman who won't take his crap.

I brush those thoughts off and turn back to my folders. One of my earlier meetings was with a previous client. I've done her living room and dining room, but now she's extending and wants a library designed to match.

The best part? It's totally a Beauty and the Beast library. You know the one. With the endless bookshelves and a ladder that swings right across? Yep. That one.

It makes me sigh every time I think of it. For all my... extracurricular activities, I love a good book. Or ten. Or one hundred.

If I had the patience or the inclination to go property hunting once more, I'd so get an apartment with room for a library.

Not to read the books, you understand. Fuck that. You don't crack spines. That's why some clever bastard created Kindles. Paperback books are the diamonds of the book world.

I mean, I sniff them. The pages smell awesome.

God. I sound like a weirdo, even in my own head.

But whatever. The point remains, Mrs. Hinsky wants me to design her a library, so design her a library I'm gonna damn well do.

"Is it common practice to work whilst lying on the floor?"

My head jerks around at the sound of his voice. "Is it common practice to enter someone's office unannounced?"

Carter looks down at his feet. "I'm not inside, Bee. And your door is open."

I glance at the floor. Ugh. He's right. "Whatever." I pull myself up to standing and slip my feet back in my shoes. "I assume you're here to collect your designs."

One of his eyebrows quirks up. "You assume correctly," he echoes my words from earlier.

"Come in." I wave in his general direction and walk across to my desk.

"Don't you have a cleaner?"

"It's not a mess. It's called organized chaos, and we happen to work incredibly well together, thank you very much." I turn just in time to catch his calculating emerald gaze sweep every inch of the room.

They finally come to rest on my desk, and he studies it almost intently until his lips tug up on one side. He looks up, our eyes colliding. "Is that why you were on your floor? A little too much 'organized chaos' on your desk?"

I snatch his file as annoyance sizzles in my bloodstream. I hand it to him over the desk. "Here's your design, Mr. Hughes. I'd show you out, but quite frankly, I don't fucking want to." I finish with a tight smile and a look that could shatter granite.

I stalk past him and gather my things from the floor. Organized chaos on my desk indeed. It's the tidiest damn space in this room because it's where I work. So what if my back aches from sitting at it for twelve hours and I wanted to lie on the floor? My office. My rules.

I put my books and pencils on the wooden surface of my desk and look up. Carter is still standing in front of it, his eyes intense, his lips quirked, and his general presence almost intimidating. He stares at me with a look I can only describe as hungry, and the shivers that cascade down my spine are enough to make me fight a full-body shiver.

"I can't help but notice you're still here," I comment, lifting an eyebrow in challenge. "Is there something I can help you with? Perhaps a direction to the door?"

He doesn't respond.

I lift my arm and point to the door. "Make a one-eighty turn, approximately twenty steps forward, turn left, then keep walking until I can shut the door without you in here. Clear enough?"

"Is this how you treat all your clients, Ms. Donnelly?"

"No." I match the intensity of my gaze to his. "Only the ones I don't like."

"Funny. You liked me enough when my cock was in your mouth."

"I also liked you when your head was between my legs, but you don't see me throwing that around like it's fucking candy on Halloween."

He tilts his head to the side and pats the file that holds his designs. "Thank you for this."

"I'd say you're welcome, but my mother raised me to tell the truth. So...." I shrug with a smile.

He turns, the folder tucked under his arm, and walks to the door. I let out a long breath as he approaches it and grab my desk chair.

My door slams.

I jerk my head up.

And Carter Hughes is storming toward me, his eyes burning with feral desire.

He drops the file on my desk, grabs my wrist, and yanks me against the wall. A small cry leaves me as my back collides with the cold surface, but he flattens his body against mine and grabs my face with his hands. The way he tilts my head back is rough; but the kiss is even rougher.

His lips move against mine with the force of a wild hurricane flying through the skies. It's raw and uncontrolled—a series of desperate movements that have my whole body burning.

His strong hands grasp mine and pin them above my head. Once again, he has me at his mercy, and I'm nothing but a victim as his desire attacks mine in the most brutal way.

Except I like it.

God, as our lips dance against each other's and my heart pounds beneath him, I like it.

Somehow, I manage to pull away, and I breathe in deeply. "Do you always

47

kiss people you could potentially hire?"

"Only the ones I don't like," he retorts.

Fucking smartass.

His lips fall back onto mine as soon as the final word has left his body, and I'm helpless once again.

The man has the mouth of the devil, and he tastes exactly like sin.

I manage to wrench my wrists from his grip and push him away. I step to the side—well, stagger, whatever—and touch my thumb to my lower lip. I can feel it's swollen from him, and my chin is raw from the stubble that coats his. "You should leave. Now."

"I've heard a variation of those words before."

"I mean it. Leave. Now." My heart is thundering against my ribs, the pounding of my blood so intense that I can hear it thrumming in my ears almost deafening. My clit is aching like a motherfucker and my pussy is practically screaming at me that I'm a stupid bitch, but no.

No damn way is it going that far again.

No horizontal tango, no wall waltz, and definitely no bending over a table sex.

Carter stares at me for a long moment, and I can't help but glance down. His erection is straining against his black pants. My tongue flicks out and sweeps across my lips, wetting them. His gaze darkens as he registers the movement.

He takes three slow, calculated steps toward me. My lungs burn with the harsh breath I take, and I keep my gaze trained on him in warning.

No more kissing.

That is not professional at all.

He reaches onto my desk and takes the file containing his designs and tucks it under his arm. Without another word, he walks across my office, side-stepping a half-fallen pile of design magazines. Tension hands heavy in the air as he moves for the door handle and pushes it down.

"If you need to discuss anything, my card is in there. It has my direct number on it," I say quietly, my hand now clasping my throat. "If I don't answer, leave a message. I try to get back to everyone within an hour."

He nods his head sharply. "You'll have an answer within twenty-four hours, Ms. Donnelly, either way."

"Thank you. Good night, Mr. Hughes."

He turns his face to me, his eyes glinting with something indiscernible. "Good night, Ms. Donnelly."

Silence reigns as he closes the door behind him, and I can't help but think that I've just sealed my fate.

I can only think one thing.

My mother is going to kill me.

CHAPTERSIX

My office door swings open and my mother steps through the empty space, standing formidably tall. A frown mars her usually wrinkleless forehead, and she zeroes in on me instantly. "Bee!"

"What did I do now?"

She reaches behind her and slams my door with such a force that it bounces open before settling against the frame. She gives it one last shove and it clicks shut. "I was just on the phone with Carter Hughes."

Oh sweet fuck. Here we go.

I may as well say goodbye to my ovaries because I think I'm about to shit them out.

"Everything okay?" I ask nonchalantly.

"Do I sound like everything is okay?" she retorts sharply.

I get the feeling that's a rhetorical question.

"He informed me you were incredibly rude during your meeting yesterday." Mom smacks her lips together. "Care to explain yourself?"

"He's a very frustrating man," I answer carefully. "And as for rudeness, people in glass houses shouldn't throw stones."

"Bee!" Mom snaps. "You can't be rude to a potential client like him!"

"Then he shouldn't be rude to me!"

"Bee…"

"No, Mom." I shut down the website I was on and focus on her fully. "We have a way of business—one that we both decided on. He wanted me to drop off the designs and I refused. I had rescheduled appointments I needed to be at. I told him to come here, and when he did, he was like a petulant child." And I was like a dog with a bone, but I'm hardly going to mention that.

Mom sighs and pinches the bridge of her nose. "Either way, he's requested you meet him at six p.m. at his restaurant. I told him you'd be there."

I wrinkle my nose. "How do you know I don't have other plans?"

"Do you?"

I'm not sure my mother will count a movie night with Charley as 'other plans.' "Yes, actually."

"A date?"

Again… I'm not sure Charley counts. "Sure. I just had a new vibrator delivered."

"Bee!" She steps back, a look of revulsion on her face.

Clearly my mother hasn't experienced the wonders of a battery-operated boyfriend. No wonder she's so uptight.

Also, a perk of having the kind of name that can't be shortened? It's really not threatening when it's yelled at you like that.

"What? I'm just being honest."

"Well, don't. Behave yourself tonight and try not to alienate Carter Hughes. You probably have just enough manners left in your body to convince him why your design is best."

And failing that, I have a mouth, a hand, and a vagina, but I'm sure she wouldn't appreciate that comment. "Sure. I'll try my best."

She pauses, as if she weren't expecting me to respond so amicably. "All right, then. Try not to alienate any other clients between now and then." She turns toward the door.

I salute her behind her back and turn back to my screen, her words flowing in one ear and out the other.

I haven't alienated a client yet.

Except perhaps Carter Hughes.

But let's be real. He was a conquest way before he was a client… at least in my world.

—◦◦◦◦◦—

Charley tilts her head to the side, repeatedly capping and uncapping her water bottle. "Do you think he's going to offer you the contract?"

"I've been to his restaurant twice. The first time, I screwed him. The second time, he told me the numerous ways we should repeat our first meeting." I frown at the bottle. Jesus, that's annoying. "I think his order for me to meet him has more to do with the fact he slammed me against a wall and kissed me last night opposed to a contract."

"Huh. You may as well run away if he doesn't offer you the contract. Your mom will lose whatever sanity she has left."

I groan and knock my head against the window of the booth we're sitting in in the cafe. "I know. What's wrong with me, Charley? Why can't I keep myself under control?"

"Uh, he kissed you." She clicks the bottle again.

I snatch it from her and slam it on the table. Thank God. "I know that. I'm just saying that maybe I should have, you know, pushed him away from me sooner."

"Like a slap to the face?"

I was thinking a little less violent, but it works. "Something like that."

The waitress brings Charley's sandwich and my Caesar salad over and sets them on the table. We thank her, and then Charley focuses on me. "Did he specify the reason for the meeting?"

"No!" I furiously stab at a piece of chicken with my fork. "Mom would have said. Just that he wants to see me tonight. Outside of office hours. In his restaurant. Alone."

She shrugs and bites into her sandwich. "So tell him you can't go," she says around the food in her mouth.

I frown at her then shake my head. "I can't do that. What if it is for work?"

"Then he should use his words and tell you that." She snorts. "Honestly, Bee. Just call him and find out."

"Like he called me?" Yeah—it hasn't escaped my notice that I gave him my direct number on the card, and he called my mother to bitch about me. I know why he did it. He's trying to get under my skin, because clearly, my panties aren't enough.

I want to call him. Then again, I also want to go and give him the cold shoulder for his dumbass tactics. The man is what—in his thirties? And he acted like an eight year old who had a pinecone thrown at their head or something.

Ugh. Professionalism is hard when personal issues get in the way. And without a doubt ours are in the way here.

I almost hope he's called and wants to meet to tell me he isn't hiring me. Almost. Because, then, hey… if he kisses me again, who am I to refuse?

The man can kiss. And do the rest of it.

This is why I shouldn't be in business. I should be stacking shelves at Target or something. Maybe answering phones in a doctor's office. Something where it doesn't matter if I screw anyone because the worst they could be is someone I'll pass again.

Jesus.

We finish the rest of our dinner in silence, and I glance at my wrist. My watch reads almost five forty-five. Crap.

"Can I leave my share?" I ask Charley. "I have to run."

She grabs my hand and looks at my watch. "Only if you call me the second you leave and tell me everything."

"Even if it's personal?"

She grins. "Especially if it's personal."

"Fine." I dig in my purse for my wallet and throw down twenty five bucks. "I'll speak to you later."

"Damn right you will." Her eyes glitter with laughter as I get up and walk away. It takes everything I have not to flip her the bird over my shoulder.

I flag a cab once I'm outside and slip into the back seat, then direct him to *Carter's*. I take a deep breath to try and center myself. Butterflies are fluttering around my stomach, and I feel like I could easily throw up at any moment. Not knowing what Carter wants with me has plagued me all day, and that's exactly why I called Charley for dinner. I hoped that being with her would take my mind off it but I was wrong.

So wrong. God. I have no idea how I'm going to get through this.

I don't want to admit how badly he affects me. He does. With his dark smirk and his arresting eyes, not to mention that sharp stubbly jaw and powerful grip... I want to melt as soon as he walks into a room. Only my own defiance stops me.

On the agenda for today: no melting.

Geez, I just don't do this crap around men.

The cab stops outside *Carter's*. I pay the driver then get out of the car. My heels click against the pavement as I walk toward the restaurant. It's almost full, and I hesitate before opening the door.

This is a stupid idea.

Which is exactly why I close my fingers around the handle and pull the door open.

I never claimed to be fucking smart, did I?

"Welcome to Carter's," the hostess greets me. "Can I take your name, party size, and time of reservation?"

"Oh," I manage. "Actually, I'm here to see Mr. Hughes. He's expecting me. Bee Donnelly."

She purses her lips. "One moment please." She turns and disappears, walking in the direction of the bar door.

It's always one damn moment in this place, isn't it?

I so badly want to drum my fingers against the countertop of the host's area or tap my foot against the floor. Don't these people know I have an important meeting with Netflix and Bert the Battery Boyfriend tonight?

I do. A very long and important meeting. I might even switch out Netflix for PornHub to spice this shit up.

The hostess comes back and offers me another tight smile. "Mr. Hughes is through in the bar. He's asked that you go straight through. He's in booth one waiting for you."

Of course he is. Of all the booths, it has to be that one.

"Thank you." I smile back at her and clutch my purse to my body. I walk through the restaurant, feeling oddly conscious of the way I look. When Carter said he caters to primarily an exclusive clientele, I didn't think he meant carats upon carats of diamonds and billionaire exclusive.

Then again, this is New York City. I've lived here my whole life and barely scratched the surface of the city's wealth.

I push open the door to the bar and blink a few times to adjust to the much lower light. I should turn around right now and leave, because there's no way a professional conversation can happen here. Especially not in that booth.

So why do my feet force me to walk alongside the black glass bar and pass every booth on the way?

Most of them have their curtains wide open, and I can just about make out figures behind the thick yet gauzy curtains.

Sweet fuck on a backseat. Could people see us at the weekend? Holy shit. I think they could—not clearly, but well enough. Oh God.

How the fuck didn't he tell me about that? How could he not? Jesus! Now I'm pissed. Did he not think to bring that up at any point in our conversation?

With a renewed vigor, I storm the rest of the length of the bar and find booth one. The curtains are pulled back, and Carter is sitting in one corner. His phone is held against his ear and he holds one finger up to me.

Oh, he didn't just do that.

He did.

I narrow my eyes. Unwillingly, I find myself exploring the way he looks. He's relaxed back, his jacket discarded on the leather seat next to him. The top two buttons of his shirt are undone, his tie unknotted but hanging around his neck. A glass of amber liquid is clasped in his hand and resting on his knee.

"Yes… Thank you. Goodbye." He pulls the phone from his ear, taps the screen, and sets it on the table. Slowly, he looks up and meets my eyes. An easy smile spreads across his lips. "Thank you for coming, Ms. Donnelly. Or is it Bee today?"

I raise one eyebrow. "Is this meeting professional or personal?"

"Professional." He smirks.

"Then it's Ms. Donnelly."

"Then have a seat, Ms. Donnelly." He motions to the chair. "Can I get you something to drink?"

"A glass of water will be fine, thank you." I sit down, sliding the skirt of my dress beneath my thighs, and set my purse next to me.

"Are you sure? I seem to remember you enjoying the wine."

Does he want my purse in his face? "I don't drink during meetings, but again, thank you."

He studies me for a second, his gaze almost making me squirm, but I hold steady under his scrutiny. "As you wish." He waves his hand and catches a server. He orders my water and another of his drink. Silence lingers between us as the drinks are made and brought to us.

"Thank you," I say to the girl who sets my water on the table.

She smiles and passes Carter his drink. "Is that all, sir?"

"Yes. Please ensure we aren't disturbed."

She nods her head once and backs out of the booth, then reaches for the curtains.

"Oh!" I stop her, extending a hand. "Please leave the curtains. Unless the meeting is a private one?" I turn to Carter, raising a questioning eyebrow.

"Ms. Donnelly," he says smoothly, "If this were private, we'd be in my office, don't you think? Leave the curtains, if Ms. Donnelly feels more comfortable this way, Bianca."

There's a spark in his eye… One that's daring. He's pushing me to see how far he can make me go.

It's written all over his face. In the twitch of his eyebrows, the curve of his lips, the intensity of his startling eyes… He wants to see how far he can take me before I break.

He's playing a dangerous, dangerous game.

Good thing I know the rulebook.

"On second thought," I say slowly, my eyes never leaving Carter's, "Close the curtains. After all, people will hear me if I scream. Isn't that right, Mr. Hughes?"

Bianca doesn't move for a moment until Carter snaps, "Close the curtains!" They close quickly and she retreats, leaving us alone. Carter turns to me and sits up, then sets his glass on the table, his eyes blazing. "You're very right. People can hear you scream. But only if I want them to. Remember that."

I level him with a steady gaze. "Please get to the point of this meeting, Mr. Hughes."

Our stare lasts a minute longer before he breaks it and leans forward. He rests his elbows on his knees and clasps in hands in front of him before looking up at me. "You're very skilled. Your design for the restaurant is exceptional."

I run my tongue across my lower lip. "Thank you."

He takes a deep breath and rubs his chin. His thumb brushes across his lips. "But I have a big problem."

I try not to let my heart drop at those words. Despite my own protests, I do want this contract. I love the concept I created.

"I'm not sure I can resist you," he admits.

I snap my eyes to his.

"Does my admission surprise you?" he asks, tilting his head. "I thought it was somewhat obvious myself."

"No… I'm surprise you admitted it," I answer honestly.

"I see no reason to lie about my attraction to you, Ms. Donnelly. One of us may as well throw out the denial."

"Are you suggesting I'm in denial?"

"Yes."

I cross one of my legs over the other and lean forward. "You'll be disappointed to learn that I'm not in denial where my attraction to you is concerned, Mr. Hughes. I can't help but feel that we're veering away from the point of this conversation, though."

"On the contrary, we're right on point. Our mutual attraction is the reason we're here. If you were anyone else I'd have called and hired you after merely glancing at your design."

"So why haven't you called and told me you don't want me to do it?"

"Because that isn't true. I want to hire you. I want to hire you a whole fucking lot, but I don't know if I trust myself to keep our relationship strictly professional. I can't help but want you."

I suck my lower lip into my mouth and bite down on it. This makes it so complicated. God... I have no idea what I'm supposed to say to him now.

It would be easier if I could promise him I can keep it professional, wouldn't it?

Problem is... if he can't... I'm not sure I can. I'm not sure how strong my refusal would be.

"What do you suggest we do?" I ask him, reaching for my water and sipping to wet my throat.

"I was hoping you had an idea."

"Opening the curtains would be a good start," I reply dryly.

His lips twitch up and he sits back. "Go ahead. I won't stop you. Neither will I seduce you with them shut."

"You're incredibly confusing. Has anyone ever told you that?"

He laughs. The rich sound is like a warm hug. "All the time. My mother insists I stole that trait from my sister who is much easier than I am."

"No. I don't believe you," I answer flatly.

He smiles. It's the most genuine smile I've ever seen from him. "Izzy drops by often. She was the one who convinced me to have this conversation with you. She's not much older than you are, and has always had a much clearer outlook than I have."

I don't know what I'm more surprised about—the fact he has a sister around my age or that he discussed us with her. "You... you told her what happened between us?"

"Not in so many words. She actually guessed and refused to accept my denials, so there we go." He holds his hands out and picks up his glass.

My mouth goes dry. Holy shit. This is not how business meetings usually go.

Damn my pussy! This is all her fault!

"I think I'll go for that wine after all," I manage to rasp out. "Excuse me."

"I can get—"

"No," I argue. "I could do with a moment alone. Thank you, though." I slide out of the booth with my purse and through the curtains, leaving him staring after me. It feels as though he's watching long after I step out of his line of sight.

I guess this meeting is both professional and personal.

I take a deep breath and smile as Bianca rubs her hands on a towel and comes to me. "Could I get a glass of wine, please? Blush zinfandel."

"Sure thing. On Mr. Hughes' tab?" she queries, glancing back as she pulls a bottle from a fridge.

"Yes," Carter's voice travels across the bar.

I turn. He's standing in the doorway of the booth, watching me. Fuck me, someone doesn't know what the words 'I need a moment' mean, do they? "I'll pay you, thank you." I pull twenty dollars from my wallet and put it on the bar. Bianca takes it as smoothly as she sets my glass down. She rings it up on the register and hands me back my change. I smile in thank you and sip from my glass.

The cold, fruity taste is welcomed. So, so welcomed.

"I have a call to make," Carter tells me, coming right up to me. "I'll be around five or ten minutes. You're welcome to wait in the booth."

I nod and walk past him without a word. Honestly, I have nothing to say right this second. I really do need this time to process what he's just said to me because I wasn't expecting it. I wasn't expecting his bluntness and his raw honesty.

I wish I'd fucked up the design. I wish I hadn't been so goddamn determined and that I'd just put whatever down. I wish I'd never given him a reason to contemplate hiring me.

I should have known better.

I should know a lot of things I clearly don't.

I sink into the cold leather seat of the booth and lean back. After one more mouthful of my wine, I set the glass on the table and close my eyes. I pinch the bridge of my nose as if it'll help me clear my mind.

I can sit here all I like and think about I should have done, but there's shoulda, woulda, coulda for a reason, isn't there? The amount of times I've said that to Charley is unreal, and now here I am, smack bang in the middle of a big ass motherfucking shoulda, woulda, coulda situation.

Really, it isn't hard to decide what to do. I have to tell Carter that I'm real sorry, but I don't think this professional relationship will work. If that means the wrath of my mother, then so be it. Fact is, this time, I know what the right choice is, and this is it.

We can't work together. That was proved last night when he kissed me.

When he kissed me. Fuck, and he kissed me. The first time ever.

The worst thing about that kiss, the very worst thing?

He kissed me like he meant it.

There are a thousand types of kisses. Casual pecks. Teasing brushes. Lingering touches. Deep kisses. Slow and easy. Frantic and desperate. Pleading. Sad. Happy. Needy.

But the kisses that have meaning behind them? They're the most horrendous things ever.

Give me a sloppy, drunken, lips, teeth, and tongue kiss over one that has meaning behind it any day.

I open my eyes and focus on my wine glass. I register his presence immediately but avoid making eye contact. Instead, I reach for my glass and take a mouthful.

Silence hovers between us. It feels oddly comfortable, but I can sense the undercurrent of tension just fizzling away. It's a niggling sensation, like that of an itch just starting. I'm trying so hard to ignore it but it's almost impossible.

"Are you all right?"

His voice rumbles over my skin, but I fight the shiver it elicits. "I was just thinking," I respond quietly. I grasp my glass with two hands and rest it on my legs, then look into it. "About what you said."

"You don't have to decide anything right now. I just wanted to be honest with you. I want to hire you—like I said, your skills are exceptional—but I don't know if I can," he says in a low voice.

I give into the allure of his tantalizing gaze and turn my face to meet his. The brutal truth reflecting back at me makes my stomach flip. "I don't know if I can work with you, Carter," I say softly. "I'm not in the habit of working with my... acquaintances."

His lips twitch. "Neither am I. But this decision is yours. I just know that I had a taste of you last night and fuck, I want to kiss you so badly right now."

I swallow. Hard. "You and I both know how inappropriate that would be."

"Exactly." His nostrils flare. "If you agree, then I'm certain I'll need you to resist me because I'm damn sure I can't you."

"What?" My eyebrows draw together in a frown. "I'll need to resist you? How about if I agree to this then you respect me enough to keep your cock under control?"

"Will you sass me like that through the project, Bee?"

"My personality reflects the name, remember? Bright and sharp. You bet your fine fucking ass I'm going to sass you if you're going to be an asshole."

His lips pull up on one side into a devastatingly sexy smirk that sends lust bolting right through my pussy. "It's your choice. You make the final decision. I don't need an answer today." He pulls a card from his pocket and slides it across the table. "Think on it and call me tomorrow."

I take the card and give it a glance. "What if I don't have a decision made tomorrow?"

"Then call me the next day."

I look from him and back at the card. His name and his personal number as well as the restaurant's is on it. "Thank you, but no thank you." I put the card back down and push it back to him with two manicured fingernails. "I think we both know we'll be wasting each other's time if we attempt this. I don't play pretend business well with others—least of those whose cocks have been halfway down my throat."

"Excellent. Then you won't mind if I do this." He pounces on me before I can say a word.

I'm trapped against the seat by his hard body, and I shudder when he takes a fistful of my hair and tugs my face back. His hot breath cascades across my lips and I inhale sharply. I look up through my lashes, but the pressure of his mouth falling onto mine has them fluttering shut.

I reach up and wrap his silky tie around my hands, effectively holding him against me. God, he tastes so fucking good. Like whiskey and sin… rich and forbidden.

It doesn't stop me flicking my tongue against his mouth and fighting a smile when he bites my lower lip then soothes the sting with his. It doesn't stop my pussy clenching or my clit throbbing or my nipples hardening. It doesn't stop the endless bolts of desire ricocheting around my body at light speed. No, it only heightens it.

The fact that I know I shouldn't be doing this makes it feel even better. It's so wrong but it feels so right. And I can't stop. Fuck me, I can't stop no matter how much I know I need to.

He tugs my head back. The sting from his action assaults my scalp, but it's the good kind of sting. He drags his lip along my jaw and up to my ear. "Take the job," he breathes. "Take it, Bee."

"The position we're in does nothing but convince me to stand by my refusal," I whisper. My heart is pounding frantically, doing its best to keep me alive beneath this man's deadly assault.

Carter runs his hand up along my thigh, over my skirt, and it finally comes to rest on my waist. His breath flits across my neck, and I close my eyes again at the warmth. "What if I say this—once more? You and me. Right now. Kill the tension between us and then that's it."

"On what planet does that make sense? Sure—let's give into temptation and hope it goes away." I let go of his tie and turn my face to him. He pulls back so our eyes meet, and I shake my head. "Sorry, Carter. I don't ride the same bull twice."

He eases his hand up my body, his palm brushing across my breast, until he's cupping my chin. "You're not leaving until you agree."

"I thought you said it was my decision."

"I'm a fucking liar. Say yes now and we're done. Say yes after one more fuck and we're done. Which one is it?"

Talk about a rock and a hard place.

But I did have that conversation with Ms. Greedy Pussy and tell her we're only playing with Bert the Battery Boyfriend… Then again, Bert doesn't offer much in the way of dirty talk or oral…

So I do something I might regret in the morning and give him my answer.

***

"You turned him down? Are you insane?" Charley cries, slamming her hands on my desk.

I throw a pen at her. "Shut your mouth!" I hiss. "Yes, I turned him down. What else was I supposed to do? Tell him I'd fuck him and then give him the inevitable answer? Don't be dumb!"

"Girl! Sex! Real penis!" She slaps her hand against her forehead. "I know you'd feel like you were cheating on Bert, but come on. He dies on you all the time."

"Only because I keep buying store brand batteries," I argue. "I'm cheap, what can I say?"

"She says while wearing seven hundred dollar shoes," she mutters. "Whatever. Did you tell your mom yet?"

"That I got the contract? Sure. It was the first thing I said to her this morning. She shit a unicorn and then peed out rainbows she was so excited."

"I guess your hippy dad's ways rubbed off on her after all."

I snort. Hippy Dad is currently in Mexico, probably delivering drugs for a cartel but smoking half of them on the way. "Whatever. Look—it's simple. Carter is closing the restaurant next Thursday and then I have ten days to get it back together. I don't have to see him until then, and then it's only briefly."

Yeah. After I told him there'd be no sex happening last night, we agreed terms of the contract. The written copy should be on my desk later today, but the long and short of it is that we'll spend no longer than ten minutes in each other's company unless someone else is there. Clearly his cock has a mind of its own, and we all know my vagina is a rule-breaking slut, so if we aren't alone together, shenanigans can't be shenaniganed.

It's foolproof. Like kids' medicine bottles, which I still can't get into at twenty-six. Also note that Charley's five year old niece can break into them like a pro, so foolproof is apparently only for people who can think for themselves.

Basically, I don't think it'll work. I think it's fucking stupid, but I can't have the man kissing me like that all the time. It's like... Gah. Ugh. Fuck my life. Grr. Roar. Fuck! Yeah... that sums the craziness up, doesn't it?

It just has to work this way.

"You don't honestly think this is going to work, do you?" Charley asks me, one eyebrow raised so high it's practically disappeared beneath her bangs.

"I'm trying to keep a positive outlook on the situation," I tell her. "I only have to spend seven days around him with minimal contact, and then I can go back to having my life the way it was before." Just with a lot less sex. I'd hate for this to happen for a second time, after all...

Charley stares at me. "Sweetie, you're deluded."

"I know." I sigh heavily and drop forward on my desk. "The hell am I supposed to do, Charley? I had to say yes. I couldn't not. He made that perfectly clear."

"Yeah, I figured as much." She smacks her lips together. "Just so you're aware, I'm making this disclaimer: As your best friend, I've told you that you're a fucking idiot and that I don't agree with this, even in the name of business, but I will be here when it all comes falling down with a card that says 'I told you so, douchedick.' Are we clear?"

"Perfectly. Now fuck off. I have to work."

CHAPTER SEVEN

*I*n the past seven days, I've ordered everything I need to overlook the renovation of the restaurant. I've spent endless hours on the phone to suppliers and companies and artists. Turns out Carter Hughes has a pretty bottomless wallet and wanted to commission a number of original images for the walls opposed to me buying generic ones from a store.

Apparently he likes to be unique.

Anyway, that's accumulated in four different images from the same artist, triple his usual price, and I'm to collect them on the final day of the redecorating. I agreed simply because I had no other choice.

I have a feeling the artist, Kevin Peters, won't be sleeping very much.

Now I'm on my way to the restaurant and hoping that everything will be removed and I'll be walking into what is essentially a blank canvas. That's what Carter promised me on the phone yesterday at the very least.

I'm hoping he was telling me the truth.

I'm also hoping the flooring guys are there, ready to rip up the old linoleum floor. I don't have the time to wait for them. I'm about to go into crazy bitch mode like I always do. Thankfully the guys I work with on a regular basis are more than aware of this and tend not to judge me. Most of the time at least.

I sigh as I step out of the cab. Thankfully there are vans parked up outside the restaurant, and instantly, my anxiety eases. Someone's here at least. I can deal with that. Someone's better than no one, after all.

I run my fingers through my hair, pushing it back from my face. The main door to the restaurant is open, and I clutch both my purse and my file to my chest tightly as I take a step through. All the furniture has been removed, except the host's counter and the bar. I'm almost certain they're coming out after the flooring though, so I'm not too worried on that.

"Bee!" Dave Baxter, one of my usual builders and life-long friend, comes up to me covered in dust.

I take a step back. "Don't even think about hugging me, you dusty bastard," I laugh, holding my hands up.

He stops, a grin stretching across his face. "Wouldn't dream of it, darlin'."

I drop my purse and file on the bar after sidestepping a tool box or two. Or three. "Talk me through the plan once again."

He wipes his forehead with his hand and launches into it. I listen as he goes from floors to walls to bars to tables and everything else in between. "After that, it's down to your decorators, darlin'. Mr. Hughes only designated four days to us so we're workin' on a tight schedule."

"Got it. Do you have enough time to do everything?"

"Sure we do. When have I ever let you down, Bee?"

I pat his arm, then when I step back, I look at my hand. Yep. Dusty. Ugh. I flap it around until it looks like it's clean of the pesky dirt. "I know, I know. Never. This is just a big contract and I want to make sure it's all done correctly."

Dave grins widely as I turn to my folder and flip the front cover open. "That all, huh?"

Raising one eyebrow, I flick my gaze back to him. "What else would it be?"

"Rumor has it the boss is handsome and rich."

"Let me guess… You've been speaking to Charley."

He holds his hands up. "Maybe, but everyone knows who Carter Hughes is, Bee. He's no Superman."

The clearing of a throat sounds from the door, and we both turn. And standing there, of course, is Carter Hughes, suited and booted in all his manly glory.

Awesome.

"Ah, but I could be Clark Kent." Carter smirks, stepping into the restaurant. He glances around. "I see you waste no time."

"No time to be wasted when you're on a tight schedule," I respond tightly. "Mr. Hughes, this is Dave Baxter, the lead builder on the project. Dave, this is Carter Hughes."

The two men shake hands and exchange pleasantries.

"Got a minute to talk me through what you're doing?" Carter asks him.

"Sure thing. Bee?" Dave looks at me.

"You guys go ahead. I'm gonna check I've got everything where it should be." I smile and wave them off, turning back to my folder, finally.

Really should have asked for them to keep a stool for me. Christ. Standing in four inch heels is no joke. I flick through my designs for the restaurant, now blocked off into areas, and check everything against the schedule.

My mom always says I have a funny way of organizing everything. She's adamant that the phrase 'organized chaos' was created for me and me alone, mostly because my files and folders and indeed, office, make little sense to anyone other than me. I could find a week old pencil sharpening in my office while most people would struggle to find my computer. It's just how I work.

I like a little craziness. I think everyone should have a little bit of reckless, crazy chaos in their life. It makes things exciting.

I shift my weight from foot to foot as I study everything. Before I know it, I've taken the bar over with my sheets and calendars and snapshots.

Damn. I need one of these bars in my office. Actually, ten. I need like ten. Complete with alcohol and glasses… Actually, scratch that. Alcohol wouldn't come in bottles if it was meant for glasses. Right?

Right.

That's my story and I'm sticking with it.

Okay, Bee. Time to focus on the job at hand.

By the time it takes Dave and Carter to do a walk-through of the restaurant and for Dave to explain all the timings to Carter, there isn't an inch of the old wooden bar top left visible, and I have my neon Sharpies starring and circling things like I'm a toddler with a blank piece of paper and mommy's pens.

I get a lot of glee out of my neon Sharpies, okay?

Carter frowns at me, still shifting side to side. "Everything all right?"

"Hmm?" I question, underlining a prospective phone call with a fluorescent yellow line.

"You're moving like you're five years old and the teacher won't let you use the bathroom," he responds dryly.

Dave snorts.

I throw my Sharpie lid at him, but he catches it, and I realize what I just did. "Oh, shit! I need that!" I take it from his hand and shove it on the end of my pen. I wave it at him. "Thanks, sweetie. Your old baseball catching skills came in real useful here."

Dave rolls his eyes, and instantly, Carter's narrow. "You two know each other well?"

"Sure," I answer, starring something on the sheet. "We went to school together. I'm not allowed to use anyone else for projects or he'll hunt me down."

"I didn't say hunt you down. Besides, you wouldn't dream of using anyone else." Dave winks.

I grin. "I know. And since you've forgotten, you still owe me dinner from the last project."

He groans. "I thought *you'd* forgotten."

"I'm like an elephant, Dave. You should know that. I never forget anything— unless it's the price of shoes."

He drops his eyes to my feet. "Obviously."

I poke my tongue out and cap my pen. "I pay for that in pain, okay?"

"And that's why she's dancing like a kindergartener desperate for a pee," Dave tells Carter.

A very annoyed Carter. "Are there no stools or chairs left?"

"Nope. All cleared out this morning on her orders." Dave crooks his thumb toward me.

"Yeah, yeah. Whatever. I didn't plan to be here all day. I have to swing by Kevin Peters' studio and check on the progress of his pictures, call the decorators to make sure the wallpaper will be here tomorrow, and then the electricians to see if my light fixtures are in." I glance at my planner. "Oh, and speak to the tilers about the bathrooms to bring them up to date modernly like we talked about," I say to Carter with a fleeting look. "And then I was going come back and berate you all for not tearing the floor up quickly enough," I tease Dave, fighting my smile.

"You really need to hire an assistant," he mutters.

"Why would I hire an assistant for things I can do myself? You've met Carlos. I asked him to order me a bookshelf last week and he had a wine rack delivered."

"How did he do that?" Carter asks, his shoulders taut.

I shrug. "God knows. Asking him to do anything is like asking a toddler to do algebra and getting a picture of a monkey with three heads. Anyway. Point is—I don't need an assistant." Movement behind Dave has me sitting up straight. "Dave, tell Dan that if I see him screwing around again I'm going to take a piece of this flooring and insert it firmly between his ass cheeks."

Dave turns and seeing the younger guy messing around, groans. "Dan!" he hollers, walking across the restaurant.

Carter leans around me and grabs my planner.

"Do you mind?" I ask, reaching for it.

He steps back without taking his eyes off the pages. "Not at all."

I narrow my eyes as he continues to peruse it. "What are you doing?"

"You know Julia can help you with this, don't you?" He lifts the spotted planner and looks at me. "She can go and check on Kevin Peters and probably check on the wallpaper. Since we're closed she has a lot less work to do."

"Again, I don't need an assistant, so thank you, but no thank you." I take the book back from him and set it on the bar.

"Don't you trust her? She organizes me efficiently."

"And I'm sure she does a great job at that, but I just like to handle things myself."

"Ahhh," he says in a low voice, joining me at the bar. He rests his forearms on the top and leans forward, turning his face toward me. "You're a control freak."

"I am not a—" I pause when I realize just how close he is to me, "control freak," I finish. I look away from him and focus on my planner so I don't accidentally drop my eyes to the way his white shirt is hugging his muscular arms.

"Are you sure?"

"Wanting to stop by and personally check on Kevin Peters and his progress means I'm invested in making sure my client—you—has the best possible quality of work for his business. Calling the electricians and decorators myself simply means that if there's a problem then I'm already on the phone and don't have to rearrange my whole day to make extra calls." I huff out a breath. "None of that makes me a control freak. It makes me dedicated."

"I didn't peg you for a control freak," Carter replies, amused.

"And what does that mean?" I turn back to him.

Stupid Bee. Stupid, stupid Bee.

His eyes flare. "I'd tell you, but I'm not allowed." He smirks and, with a wink, pushes off of the bar. "When are you planning to see Kevin?"

"Uh..." I shake my head to clear it from the implication of his words. "Right after I've checked that Dave has all his ducks in a row. They tend to waddle off."

"Much like your own."

"If you were anyone but my client, I'd tell you to fuck yourself," I say under my breath, slamming my planner shut and walking to Dave.

I spend the next few minutes going over everything with him before he assures me he's passed on my threat to Dan and insists I go do my thing before I break out in hives.

So I like to keep to my schedule. Just because my office looks like a department store threw up in it doesn't mean my schedule does.

Carter's leaning against the bar on his phone when I approach. He looks up, still typing. "Everything all right?"

"As all right as it can be," I respond. "I'm going to see Kevin now. He said he was free late morning. Did you want to come?"

"Sure." He presses a button on the side of his phone and slips it into his pants pocket. "You need a hand packing this up?" He waves his hand over the stuff on the bar.

I flap my own dismissively. "Just my planner. They know if they touch it then they're dead meat."

"You're a feisty boss, aren't you?" He's clearly fighting a laugh.

I raise an eyebrow. "When you're a woman surrounded by men in the workplace, being a wilting flower won't get shit done. They respect me or they don't work for me. They know that. Thank you," I add when Carter opens the restaurant door and holds it for me.

I walk to the curb and he grabs my hand. "What are you doing?" he asks me.

"Getting a cab…"

He shakes his head with a wry smile and clasps my upper arms from behind. He directs me a few feet along the sidewalk toward a sleek black Mercedes waiting at the side of the curb. He releases me to open one of the back doors and motion for me to get in.

How the other half live, eh?

Sure, Mom and I make a ton of money, but not personal chauffeur kind of money. Must be nice.

"Thank you," I say again, getting into the back seat and sliding along it.

Carter settles in on the other side and shuts the door behind him. "Where's the studio?" he asks me, leaning forward.

I give him the address and he relays it to the driver, and getting an affirmative answer, slides the partition closed. Butterflies start up in my stomach, the stupid little creatures, and I swallow in an attempt to hide my nervousness.

So much for not being alone for more than ten minutes. It's at least fifteen minutes to the studio and then a further fifteen back.

Agreement screwed already.

Fuck. I couldn't have realized this before, could I?

"Dave seems to have a handle on his team," Carter remarks, shifting so he can look at me. There's a questioning glimmer in his eyes, one that doesn't make much sense.

"I'd hope so. He's been working with some of them since he was sixteen. It's his father's business, but he sticks to the office side more often than not now. Dave unofficially runs the show," I answer.

He nods slowly. "And you've known each other since school?"

"Kindergarten. Our moms are close friends. They wasted five years trying to set us up."

"And has it ever worked?"

My eyebrows shoot up at the personal question. "We went on one date. I got food poisoning and puked on him when he went to kiss me."

Carter half-smiles. "Was that before you learned how to voice your aversion to commitment?"

"I believe that was the day I learned." I smirk. "What about you? Aren't you kind of young to have such an... exclusive... restaurant?"

"When my grandfather passed, he left me a trust fund. The only catch was that I had to invest it into property. I bought the restaurant when it was a run-down ice cream parlor when I was twenty-three and used the cash I had left to turn it around. I barely made a profit the first year."

"How'd you get from teenagers on first dates to sex in private booths?"

The grin that teases his lips is just pure sex. "I added hot food. More people started buying food than ice cream. I lived in the upstairs apartment and lived frugally. I renovated when I had enough money to get a loan from the bank two years later."

"So you were... twenty-six."

"Correct. It took three months, but when I reopened, it was with a better menu, and the area was becoming more exclusive. By the end of that year I'd paid off my loan and still had money to spare. When I was twenty-nine, I bought my house and added the bar. Four years later, I own my house outright, cater to people whose names I'm not allowed to mention in public, and have a bank account that would make many Hollywood stars weep."

"From just one restaurant?"

"No. I have several. A handful in-state, then Chicago, Boston, Denver, and Seattle. I have one opening in Los Angeles later this year."

"Impressive," I say softly. "All that from a trust fund."

"Yep. All he asked was when I made it, I'd put that money in a fund for my child or grandchild." Carter shrugs a shoulder. "Seemed fair. It'll likely go to my niece or nephew when my sister has a child. She's the fairytale lover out of us."

"What? You don't think you'll find your Cinderella? I'm shocked," I say dryly.

He chuckles. "Actually, I'm pretty sure I'll find her, but the chances of me returning her shoe are pretty slim. I'll just send her a check for the cost or something."

"I'd keep that to yourself if I were you."

"What would you want? The shoe or the check?"

"The shoe, and then I'd thank you and slam the door in your face." I smile sweetly.

His chuckle grows to a laugh. "And you doubted I'd find Cinderella."

I roll my eyes. "Please. My shoes are far too expensive to leave behind."

"I know. I have to buy Izzy a pair every birthday," he drawls.

The driver raps on the partition and Carter leans forward to open it. "We're here, Mr. Hughes," he says.

"Thank you. Wait, please." Carter opens the door and gets out of the car. He holds the door as I slide across the seat, then reaches down and takes my purse.

My eyebrows shoot up as I look up at him and put my hand in his offered one. He steadies me as I get out of the car and step onto the curb. He shuts the door before releasing my hand and passing me back my purse.

"Thank you," I say for a third time this trip, mildly surprised by his actions.

He smiles slowly, his green eyes reflecting a flash of amusement. "It's simple manners, Bee."

"Of course." I straighten my skirt as he reaches for the studio door and holds that open, too.

He touches his fingers to my waist as I come to walk past him and dips his head. "Some of us are still gentlemen, you know."

"Nice to know," I whisper on an inhale.

Acts like a gentleman. Talks like a wet dream. Fucks like a pornstar.

I'm. So. Screwed.

We leave Kevin Peters' studio happy, and Carter with a further two pieces commissioned, this time for his house. Apparently the man is somewhat of an art connoisseur.

Me? I just want something to eat. I'm starving.

"Are you headed back to the restaurant to make your calls or your office?" he asks me once we're in the car and heading back into Manhattan.

"The office would be great. It gets noisy when they start ripping shit up."

He nods and checks his watch. "We can stop for lunch if you'd like."

"Oh… It's okay. I'll order something in when I get to my office."

"Are you sure? I know a really great burger place." His eyebrows arch, and the upward turn of his lips are convincing.

"I'm not really dressed for a burger place," I answer. "Honestly, I'm fine. Thank you for offering, though."

He sighs and sits back. "You're one of those salad-only types, aren't you?"

"Only if I can order pizza the next day." I snort. "Trust me. I watch what I eat but I'm not obsessive. I enjoy a burger as much as the next person." I won't tell him I ate almost a whole sharing bag of tortilla chips right before we met.

"So get lunch."

I sigh softly. "That isn't a good idea, is it?"

"Why? We've been successfully alone for…" He looks at the time. "… Almost two hours."

I purse my lips. "Which is against what we agreed."

He rests his arm across the back of the seat and levels his gaze on me. "Bee, I'm not asking you on a date. I'm asking you if you'd like lunch. Fuck, argue about buying your own if it'll make you feel better. We have a working relationship and I'd never do something that'll make you uncomfortable."

I could really, really go for a burger right now. "Okay, okay. Fine. But I am paying for my own."

The smirk that accompanies his side-eyed glance as he sits forward to tell the driver where to go informs me that my argument is entirely futile, but hey.

It feels good just to make that point… Even if it was a waste of breath.

After several minutes of silence ranging from comfortably looking out of the window to awkward moments of eye contact and an almost knee-brush, we pull up outside a burger place. Once again, Carter helps me out of the car, purse and all, before shutting the door. He places a hand on my lower back and guides me into the building with a gentle push.

A shiver runs down my spine, one I can't control. His fingers twitch where his touch is burning into my skin at my side. My heart does a quick double beat as the smell of burgers assaults my senses. I do my best to focus on the rich scent, but I can't.

The sensation of his touch is just too consuming.

He keeps his hand on my back as I stutter my way through my order and make a last-ditch attempt to protest about him paying for my lunch. I only breathe easily when he lets me go to pull out his card and pay.

I take the chance to run and snag a table. I just… need to breathe. It's like he's touched me once and through his fingertips, he's drawn out every bit of oxygen I need to survive.

These feelings are insane. So what if we had one night? So what if I know all the things he wants to do to me and in all the places? Christ—this isn't okay. Why did I let him talk me into lunch?

What's it going to be next? He's going to talk his way into slipping his cock inside me?

I don't care if he is being a gentleman. I don't like him being a gentleman. I don't think I can take one more brush of his hand across any part of me, even if it's my fucking shoulder or ankle something.

Hell, don't even touch my purse, man. I'd probably shudder at that shit, too.

I need to calm down. I need to breathe. Nine more days of this—surely I can do this by avoiding him? Call ahead before I go to the restaurant or just hope he has other things to do? That works, doesn't it?

Questions, questions, questions. It's always questions with him, isn't it?

Maybe Charley was right. Maybe I'm a dumbass for not fucking him again when I had the chance, when he was offering it right there and then. Would I want him less if I did?

Should I try—

No. I shouldn't. I should not try and proposition him.

"It'll be around ten minutes," Carter says, taking the seat next to me and putting my water in front of me. "Tell me about Donnelly Designs."

I take the bottle and uncap it. "What about it?"

"How did you start it? You're part owner, right?"

Slowly, I nod. "My mom owns the majority. She started it when I left college." I run through everything, and when I'm done, our food is here.

"So your mom controls it all?"

"Kind of." I dab the corner of my mouth with my napkin and peer up at him through my eyelashes. "Thanks for calling her that time, by the way. She's still bitching at me about my supposed attitude."

His eyes glitter with restrained laughter. "My apologies. I'll make sure to follow up and tell her how talented you are."

I stare at him flatly. "Gee, that doesn't sound patronizing at all."

He grins and takes a bite out of his burger.

I kind of want to hit him in the face with mine.

Thankfully, he doesn't respond, and we finish our lunch in amicable silence. Well, I say amicable… His silence is amicable. Mine is definitely pissed off. I think I'm learning he has this effect on me.

Turns me on one minute, pisses me off the next.

We make our way outside where the car is still waiting, and I glance over it. There are an abundance of cabs, several of which look empty, and I weigh up my options—another few minutes with him in a car or get a cab?

It isn't hard to choose.

"Thank you for lunch," I say to him, tucking some of my hair behind my ear. "I need to get back to the office now, but I can check in with you later to update you."

"I'd appreciate that. Can I take you there?"

I smile coyly. "Until you're in the driver seat, you're not really taking me anywhere, are you?"

One of his dark eyebrows quirks up. "Well, any time you want me to hop into it, I'll be happy to take you wherever you want to go." His voice is husky, and fuck the goosebumps that are appearing up and down my arms. Fuck them so hard.

I step off the curb and raise my arm. A cab turns toward me almost instantly, and I grab the door handle, wrenching it open. "Noted, Mr. Hughes."

"Have a good afternoon, Ms. Donnelly."

Oh I will, I think as I get in the back seat and direct the driver to our office building. Especially since he won't be in it.

CHAPTEREIGHT

"*W*ell, that was a bust." Charley sighs and drops herself onto my snuggle armchair. Her purse falls to the floor, and she kicks her heels off.

I wince as they hit my wooden floor, heel first. "The date? Why?" I almost forgot that tonight was her second date with Carter's friend… The bastard behind my initial meeting with the man.

She groans. "He thought we'd… You know."

"Bump bulls?"

"Yes. That. I had to disappoint him because I don't have sex on the second date."

"You're on your period, aren't you?"

Another groan, but this one sounds so much more painful. "Yes! And it's like a thousand rabid woodpeckers are trying to drill their way through the walls of my uterus!"

I get up, walk to the pill drawer, and grab a packet of period pain pills. I throw them at her head. "Here, bitchypants. Take two of those."

"Thank you!" She sighs and pops two from the foil strip, then takes the glass of water I hand her. "Anyway, long story short, he was apparently only in it to get his snake in my turban and that's the end of that."

"I'm sorry. That sucks."

"Oh, you sound real sorry." She rolls her eyes.

"Hey, I tried!" I protest, sitting on the sofa and crossing my legs in front of me. "That counts for something, right?"

"S'pose," she mutters, reaching inside the front of her dress and fiddling with her bra. She slides the straps down her arms, just avoids a nip-slip, and sets her bra in her lap.

Welcome to Best Friend Ville. Population: Crazy.

If I didn't do the same thing to her, I'd be real pissed.

"I don't know why you keep trying so hard. This is New York. There are thousands of guys that actually deserve your time. All you're doing by going on these endless, useless, fucking shit dates is hurting yourself. Cinderella didn't go to her fairytale, and neither did Sleeping Beauty or Snow White. Their fairytales came to them."

"Meanwhile, Rapunzel whacked hers over the head with a frying pan," she replies dryly.

"And I am so Rapunzel," I answer. "But the point is Flynn Rider still came to her, did he not?"

"I guess." She's just grumbling now. "I already tried that though, remember?"

"Charley, you went two weeks without going on a date. That's like waiting for the flowers in your window to bloom." I roll my eyes. "Wait for them to die and come back. If it doesn't work then, then go back searching. The only dates you're finding are rotten and moldy."

"Mmm. I'll think about it. Anyway, how's the issue at work?" She rolls her face to me. "You didn't call yesterday so it can't have been bad."

I shrug and pick at a loose thread on my sock. "Yesterday was… odd, but okay. Today was the best. I didn't see him even once. Didn't even call or anything. It was like heaven."

"You're laying it on pretty thick."

"Pretty thick is exactly how I feel."

"You were alone with him yesterday, weren't you?"

Best friends. Knowing what you don't say since the dawn of time.

I tell her everything about the first day, from the trip to the artist's studio to lunch to the two minute phone call as I updated him. I was super glad not to see him today because, honestly, I don't know how much of him I can take. I think my Carter Hughes meter is getting pretty full.

I might need a vacation after this job is done. Or halfway. Whatever.

"Didn't you guys agree not to be alone?" Charley questions.

"Yep."

"And you broke it on the first morning."

"Yep."

"You know the chances of you finishing this job without kissing, sucking, or fucking him are incredibly small, don't you?"

I sigh and cup my chin with my hands. "Yep. But I'm holding onto that little chance. Like when you rush to the store when there's a sale on for those shoes you want but you know probably won't be there in your size? They're never in mine. So sex with Carter is my new coveted shoe that I absolutely won't get."

Charley pauses for a moment. "That actually makes perfect sense. Kudos."

"Thank you."

She swings her legs around the chair. "Now that's out of the way—where's the ice cream?"

Another day passes without seeing Carter.

I like it that way—always have, regardless of the client. Some can be overbearing and constantly question the way I do things. The worst one was a socialite whose husband had given her free reign with the whole house. It took months to complete, and in the end, I had to tell her husband very nicely that if he didn't whisk her off somewhere nice on vacation for the final three weeks of the project, I'd be quitting and billing him for the mental health days I'd surely require.

Thankfully, he laughed, winked, and the next day, they were on their way to Bora Bora.

Nice work if you can get it.

The restaurant is now totally bare. It's day three and the floors are up, the wallpaper is pretty much all stripped, and the bar has been demolished. There's nothing but wood, wood, and more wood. Also a bit of brick here and there. Apparently there was some cracked plasterboard beneath the paper, so that's getting fixed up first thing this morning.

I just want it to stop looking like a building site so I can get in here and go wild with the design. I keep mentally rearranging pictures and décor every time I walk into this room. I'm itching to get stuck in and tear open the boxes of things that are sitting in the storage room waiting for the rest of their friends to join them.

Like… God. I love designing, I do. But I love being in the room and seeing it finished—making it be finished.

I can see it now in this room… How to position the pictures for maximum light from the new fixtures being fitted this afternoon. How to arrange things for privacy between tables. How to lay out the centerpieces. The exact angles of tables…

Yet everything will change when all the furniture has been delivered and assembled. I know I'll change everything until I'm right back at the original design, and that's the fun of it. Also frustrating, but fun just sounds way more positive.

Satisfied with how everything is going, I tell Dave to call me if he needs anything and grab a cab outside the restaurant. I settle back into the seat on the way to the office and flick through my planner. Aside from a couple of phone calls and a home visit, the next week is dedicated solely to *Carter's*. Unfortunately, I'm a bit of a useless shit in these first few days.

I'm no wallpaper master.

I put my planner back in my purse, pay the driver, and get out of the car. The clouds are gathering in the sky above me, blocking out the sunlight and sending a slight chill through the air. I shiver at the thought of rain and head into the building. My heels click against the floor of the lobby area and I throw one of the security guys a wave before pushing the button for the elevator.

The doors open with a ping, and I get in. I jab the button for Donnelly Designs' floor and step back. The doors slowly close, and I wriggle my toes inside my shoes just as a hand slips between the doors and forces them to open.

I swallow my groan as my eyes meet the emerald green of Carter Hughes'.

I knew it was too good to be good.

"Ms. Donnelly. Fancy seeing you here," he comments smoothly, joining me inside the elevator.

"Yes, it must be so shocking, especially given that I work in this very building," I drawl.

He adjusts his sleeve at his wrist and shoots me a sideways glance, smirking. "So you do. How are things at the restaurant?"

"Looks like a toddler went into it with a bulldozer."

"Just as expected then."

I look over at him, my lips twitching. "Absolutely. Are you here for business?"

"Actually," he says slowly, turning to face me fully. "I'm here to see you."

Well, this is going to go one of two ways. "You are?"

"You sound surprised."

"I am." Thankfully, the doors ping open. I push off the back wall of the elevator, only for Carter to beat me to it and slip out. He flattens a hand against the opened door edge to stop it from closing. "Thank you."

I swear all I do is thank this man.

"You're very welcome." He smiles and follows me.

Carlos is sitting behind his reception desk, slumped forward and looking at what seems to be his Kindle.

I clear my throat.

He looks up, eyes wide. The Kindle quickly disappears. "Bee! You're back sooner than I expected."

"Obviously. Good book?" I query, walking up to the counter.

"Not bad. Could use a little less kissing and a bit more murder." He shrugs.

I just about refrain from rolling my eyes. "Do I have any messages?"

"Mrs. Cortez cancelled again and requested you call her back. Your mother said to tell her—"

"I can imagine," I cut him off. "Anything else?"

"Yes. She's at Louis' for the next two hours working on carpet and wallpaper

82

samples."

"Carpet and wallpaper samples, hmm?" I take the notecard from him with Mrs. Cortez's phone number. "Did she say if they were his current ones or future ones?"

Carlos grins. "Nope. I'm going to bet on current ones."

"I'd bet with you but it doesn't count if we bet the same thing." I turn to my office then spin back, almost bumping into Carter. "Hey, did my bookshelf arrive?"

I'd swear Carlos blushes. "It's due for delivery tomorrow."

I point the notecard at him. "And you're sure it's a bookshelf this time?"

"Your mom watched as I ordered it. Definitely a bookshelf."

"Just messing with you. Thanks." I smile and open the door to my office. "Come in, Mr. Hughes."

He follows me in and shuts the door just as I drop the card with Mrs. Cortez's number in my trashcan. "Not a fan of her?" he questions, pointing to the trash.

"She's cancelled her last four appointments. I have her number memorized at this point." I dump my purse on the floor by my chair and flatten my hands on the desk. "What can I help you with?"

He tugs on his tie, then with carefully calculated steps, closes the space between him and my desk. He rests his hands on the desk in front of mine, and for the first time, I'm thankful for the mess I have between us, otherwise I'm certain he'd make sure our fingertips touch.

He leans forward, his gaze zeroing in on mine in that compelling way he has. I'm trapped in the intensity of his stare, and there's nothing I can do but stand here and hope that my eyes aren't giving away the flip-flop feeling in my stomach.

Shit.

"I have to go to California for three days to look over some things with my restaurant opening there," he says quietly. "I wanted you to be aware that Julia will be overlooking things here, and there's a high chance my sister might just stop in to be nosey."

Awesome. "And if there's a problem?"

"Then you call me. Julia will check in with you twice a day, and as efficient as she is, I'd prefer to handle any issues myself."

"And you called me a control freak."

"You are a control freak." He leans forward even further.

I can feel his breath just ghosting across my lips. "I'm not."

"You are. It's why you dislike me so much."

"What the hell does me supposedly being a control freak have to do with liking you or not?"

"Because." He reaches one hand up and runs his thumb down my jaw. The backs of his fingers brush across my neck, and I swallow hard, drawing a tiny, knowing smile from him. "You can't control what your body does when I'm around you. When I touch you."

His hand dips over my collarbone until his fingers are dangerously close to dipping against my cleavage. I straighten, shoving off of the desk. "I have no idea what you're talking about. If that was all... I have an appointment soon."

He doesn't move. He stands there stonily, the only part of him moving his eyes. They drop to my chest and flick back up, hesitating on my mouth when I lick my lips.

He really needs to leave. He's undressing me with his eyes, for fuck's sake. No—screw that.

The man is fucking me with his eyes, and he's doing it damn well.

I take a deep breath and draw myself up to my full height. I'll show him the door. I have to show him the door.

Screw this throbbing in my vagina. She's the reason I'm in this situation. She can fuck herself later.

I stalk past Carter in the direction of the door. He's quicker than me, though. His arm darts out and his fingers curl around my wrist, and he yanks me against his hard body. The air whooshes out of my lungs as our chests collide and he secures me against him with one strong arm.

"You're doing it again," he murmurs in my ear. "Responding to me. Like I can't see it. I can. It's written all over your pretty face."

My blood, red hot, thunders through my body, and my cheeks flush. "You're seeing things," I whisper. "Please let me go." I push against him, but he only holds me tighter.

"I deliberately stayed away from you yesterday. Do you know that?" When I shake my head, he continues. "After we had lunch, I knew I couldn't be around you. You made the right choice in getting a taxi here. There's no way, had you have gotten into that car with me, that I wouldn't have smudged the fuck out of your lipstick, Bee."

I run my tongue across the inside of my teeth as I consider what to say. What am I supposed to say? "Have you considered it's perhaps best to coordinate with my mother and have her oversee this project instead of me?"

"A thousand times. But then I wouldn't get to watch you while you walk and imagine you bent in front of me and your ass with my still-red palm print on it."

Holy. What?

"It's definitely best if you coordinate with my mother," I breathe. His words have made every one of my nerves tingle, and right now, all my nerves seem to be in between my legs. "Three days." I swallow. "This is destined for disaster."

Like it always was.

"I agree," Carter agrees huskily. "So if it's destined, why not help it along its way?"

I open my mouth to protest, but he stops me with one swift movement that has his lips covering mine. The hotness of his mouth on mine shocks me, and I fall victim to his powerful and commanding movements. He pushes me back until my butt bumps my desk and I'm falling backward onto it.

He steadies me with his forceful grip. His other arm pushes stuff away until I'm properly perched on the edge, my legs open with him standing in between them. His hard cock pushes against my stomach as he leans into me and I curl my fingers around his neck.

I'm on fire. Everywhere.

He kisses me deeply, his tongue stroking mine, and there's nothing but him and the raging pound of desire as it flows through my body. He eases his fingers inside the hem of my dress and up the inside of my thigh toward my aching pussy, and I know I should stop him, but oh Jesus. I can't. My skin is tingling and my clit is throbbing in sweet anticipation of what's coming.

He grazes his teeth across my lower lip as his thumb brushes my lace panties. My muscles clench at the gentle touch, and I tighten my grip on the back of his neck. His fingers slide my thong to the side.

I drop my head back, breaking the kiss, right as he rubs his thumb over my clit and pushes one finger inside me. *Jesus. Fucking. Christ.* He kisses his way down my neck, each lingering touch only adding to the fire that is my want for him right now. Fuck, fuck, fuck.

This is wrong. This is so. Fucking. Wrong.

He's my client. It still doesn't matter that we met before. *He should not be finger-fucking me on my desk right now.*

"See?" he rasps in my ear. "You can't control this. You can't control how fucking wet you are right now—for me. But you don't want to, do you?" He pushes another finger inside me. "You might be a control freak, but only one of us has control over your body. And it sure as fuck isn't you, is it?"

I want to tell him to fuck himself, but I can't. "There's a better use for your smart mouth," I gasp as a jolt of pleasure sets my body alight.

"Better use for yours, too," he retorts, nipping the side of my neck. "Look at you, Bee. Look at the way you're riding my hand right now. What is it, baby? You want another?"

A third fingertip nudges the opening of my pussy, and my hips buck against his hand. I don't, but I do. A whimper escapes me as he pushes a third inside me. The stretching of my pussy is far more pleasurable than painful, but I still drop my head back with a gasp.

"Hush." Carter captures my mouth with his, biting my lower lip. "Your assistant out there doesn't seem too bright, but it probably wouldn't take him long to figure out what I'm doing to you."

Carlos. Oh, fuck. "We shouldn't—"

"Too late," he responds without missing a beat. He kisses me again, even deeper than before, successfully making me forget whatever argument I was about to present to him.

He plays my body. My mouth with his tongue and my pussy with his hand. I'm like clay and he's the master sculpture, each movement calculated for a perfect result—only this result is my orgasm.

And so it goes on. His fingers pumping inside me while his thumb circles my clit over and over, until my body goes taut and he forces my quiet cry into his mouth.

His fingers are still inside me as I drop my own to his hips and cup his rock hard cock with one hand. It's straining against his pants, and I'm dying to slide inside them and work his pleasure from him as easily as he just stole mine from me.

Three knocks at my door cut through the room, effectively killing any plan for continuation either of us had.

They also bring me to my senses.

"Jesus fuck!" I hiss, pushing him away from me. My pussy immediately mourns the loss of his fingers, greedy little whore, and I jump up off my desk. I have to reach under my desk to put my panties back in place. "Two seconds. I'm just with a client," I tell whoever is behind the door.

"Carlos told me it's Carter Hughes. I only need a moment," my mom's voice responds.

Oh. Fuck. No. Fuck a doodle fucking doo, hell no!

Carter does his belt up as I turn and grab a fabric swatch book from my windowsill and put it on the desk, opening it to the drapes fabric section. I jab a finger at the chair for him to sit in.

He has the biggest shit eating grin on his face, far more appropriate for a teenage boy than for a thirty-two year old man. I want to rip off my panties and hit him across the face with them in the hope it'll wipe that smile off of it.

I drop into my chair, and Carter scratches the corner of his mouth, looking at mine. I snatch up my phone and look at the screen. Shit. Lipstick smudged!

Damn it all! I knew I should have put the twelve-hour stuff on this morning.

I lick my thumb and scrub at the mark until it's disappeared. He smirks, leaning forward and grabbing a page of the book.

"Bee!" Mom knocks again.

"Jesus, this is a meeting!" I call back, snatching a pencil. "Come in if you really have to."

She does, apparently. With the same old look on her face as she always has…

That disdainful downturn of her lips as she realizes my office hasn't been tidied overnight. "What took so long?"

"Comparing curtain fabric swatches." I tap my pencil against a page of the book. "Carlos said you were with Louis."

"He double-booked," she responds, disinterested.

Read: they got done early. I wonder if she knows that I know her meetings with Louis are less of the interior design kind and more of the interior exploration kind.

"Oh, okay. What do you need? We're busy."

"Can you find these vases? Stacy Vince wants six of them for her dining room but they seem to be absolutely nowhere. I think they're commissioned pieces. I've tried to look but I can't, and she's left Carlos with three messages in as many days."

"No problem." I take the photos from her. They're held together by a paper clip. "That all?"

"Yes."

"And that had to be done right now because..."

"I'm hungry." She smiles at me and then turns to Carter, her smile becoming even more dazzling. "Carter! How are you?" She holds her hand out to him.

Inwardly, I wince. Please don't shake hands.

My mother does not need to clasp the fingers that, five minutes ago, were inside of me.

He stands and touches his left hand to her waist, then kisses her cheek. "I'm fine, Mrs. Donnelly, thank you. How are you?"

"Oh, I'm wonderful." Mom fans herself as she steps back.

Crisis averted.

"I didn't mean to interrupt, I'm sorry. I have a busy afternoon and wanted to get a bite to eat while I can. I'll leave you to it." She takes a few steps back, but Carter shakes his head.

"Please, Mrs. Donnelly. It's fine. I was just about to leave. I think we found what we were looking for, right, Bee?" He pins me with his gaze.

"Yes," I answer slowly. "If you're certain that's the one you want. It's hard to find sometimes."

"Oh, absolutely." The inflection in his word makes my heart clench with its implication. "Let me know if we get lucky." He winks, then with one final smile at my mom, he turns and walks out of the door.

I don't think he was talking about the pretend fabric.

Mom's eyebrows shoot up, and Carter's penetrating gaze is replaced by hers. "Now who are you trying to convince, you, that young man, or me?"

"Convince of what?" I look away from the door and focus on her.

"That you're ridiculously attracted to him."

"Please." I shut the fabric book and get up to put it back where it belongs. "He's very handsome, Mom, but he's also a bit of an arrogant pig."

"I see you're trying to convince me."

"I would have a response if I had any idea what in the hell you're talking about."

Mom walks up to me and pats my cheek. "I know you two met before, dear. Remember when he was here a few days ago?"

I have chills. I nod anyway.

"It was to inform me that your prior... relationship... Had no impact on his decision about the designer for the restaurant. He picked you for your credentials and not... otherwise." For the first time ever, she looks slightly uncomfortable. "I'm a little put out you didn't tell me, but I understand why."

I frown. "Why aren't you kicking my ass right now?"

She shrugs one shoulder and leaves that as her response.

"Mom. I fucked a client. Before he was a client. But still. And you're not even mad?"

She waves a hand and walks to the door. She pauses, her fingers wrapped around the handle. Her dark, curled hair bounces as she looks over her shoulder at me. "Bee, I'm not happy. I'd like to think you can remain professional and not cross the line while you're working together, but you're a grown woman and able to make your own choices."

Hello, guilt trip. I'll just go and pack my suitcase for you.

"That said…" Her ruby red lips quirk into a half smile, and one of her perfectly shaped brows arches up. "If you're do it with a client, you damn well picked a good one to do it with."

"Uh… Are you drunk, Mom?"

She shakes her head, and with that, she opens my door and disappears through it.

I swear she laughs.

She *must* be drunk.

My mother knows I had sex with Carter.

My life is officially over.

I'm twenty-six and I don't mind saying that she terrifies me. Hell yeah she does. She's usually like a viper waiting to strike, which is why, two days after our conversation, I'm shocked that she didn't uncoil herself and bite me in the ass for my actions.

If I were her, I think that's what I'd have done. I'd have gone crazy… I think. The thing about it though is that she is right. I am a grown woman and I should be able to make the right choices.

Note the usage of the word 'should.' Clearly I'm incapable of doing such a thing… as evidenced by the situation I was in right before she came back.

I just… *God.* The way he makes me feel is unlike anything I've ever known before. Every touch is the instant heat of a freshly lit match, and each pound of desire is the gentle burning of a candlewick. His touch makes me feel alive, but more than that, it makes me feel wanted.

And in the end, that's all anyone wants, isn't it? To be wanted. To feel wanted.

I've been wanted a lot. I've been lusted after and seduced and played with. I've allowed that to happen, but I've never really believed any of the guys I've been with, whether they were random one night stands or maybe casual fuck buddies. I've never sat back the next morning and thought to myself, 'Gee, they really, really wanted me, didn't they?'

I never experienced the rush of shattering self-control until I met Carter Hughes. I never knew what it was like to see resistance snap like an elastic band under too much pressure. I never thought I would... Not now.

He changed that. He's like a magnet with his own intimidating pull, and no matter what, I'm finding myself more and more drawn to him.

I don't want to be. I don't want to be drawn to him. I don't want to be the fly he catches in his web or the debris he pulls into his orbit with his gravitational pull.

Because that's what it is... Carter Hughes has his own universe. One I know nothing about except for the fact he's at the very center of it.

He just... commands everything. That's perhaps the best way to say it. He commands anything and everything around him, and it seems that simple. I'm sure it isn't. Nothing is ever simple once you scratch beneath the surface.

More and more, I'm feeling like I want to do that. I want to tear apart the layers that make him, him, and I want to scratch away the seemingly perfectness of his life.

No one's life is that great. Or maybe he's just one of the lucky ones. I don't know.

I do know that I'm pretty mad at him for talking to my mother. Seriously—I don't care how damn rich he is. I don't care how many restaurants he owns or who the hell he thinks he is. He shouldn't have done that.

Now I all but have my mother's blessing to screw the ever loving fuck out of the man once this contract is up. I'm sure she'd feel very differently if she'd walked into my office instead of knocking, but hey ho...

I click on the email tab on my Internet browser and on a new message. I type 'Carter' into the 'To' bar and his email address comes up immediately. I click on it and type 'Important meeting needed' into the subject bar, hit shift, and start my email.

Dear Mr. Hughes,

An urgent matter has just come to my attention. Please let me know when you arrive back to New York so we can schedule a meeting as soon as possible.

Best wishes,

Bee Donnelly.

I send it and reach for the Sour Patch Kids sitting on my desk. The packet crinkles as I open it and grab two or three candies. My computer pings as a new email hits my inbox.

From: Carter Hughes (chughes@hughesrestaurants.com)

To: Bee Donnelly (beedonnelly@donnellydesigns.net)

Ms. Donnelly,

I expect to arrive back around midday. Can I interest you in a late lunch? I know a place that does great salads if tomorrow is your designated takeout pizza night.

Hope you're well.

Carter Hughes

I smack my lips together as I hit reply. God... I really shouldn't agree to this, but okay. He twisted my arm the second he said 'takeout pizza.'

From: Bee Donnelly (beedonnelly@donnellydesigns.net)

To: Carter Hughes (chughes@hughesrestaurants.com)

Mr. Hughes,

I'm free for a working lunch at two p.m. Is this suitable for you?

From: Carter Hughes (chughes@hughesrestaurants.com)

To: Bee Donnelly (beedonnelly@donnellydesigns.net)

Ms. Donnelly,

That sounds perfect. I'll collect you from your office at one forty-five. I'll call ahead.

Also, consider bringing a change of underwear, otherwise I can't promise you'll be leaving with any on.

Actually, I know you won't be.

Have a good day.

My jaw drops open at his audacity. What the hell?! Who does this man think he is?

I can't even respond to that. More to the point, I have no fucking idea what I'm supposed to respond to that.

I click the 'x' in the top corner of my screen and slam my laptop shut.

Arrogant fuckwad.

CHAPTERNINE

I run the brush through my hair one last time and put it back in my desk drawer. I've been watching the clock all morning like I'm some kind of freaked out teenage girl waiting for her first date.

I want to know why he told my mom. It's been three days since she and I had that conversation, and I'm still as mad as I was then. Hell, I'm fuming. I want to take my eyelash curlers and close them around the end of his cock kind of fuming.

Fact is, I had a plan.

Get this contract.

Do the design.

Get paid.

Never. See. Him. Again.

Ergo, my mom never would have found out about our night together. Carter made it clear during our consultation that it wouldn't influence matters. He admitted he didn't want to see me again. Fuck, I didn't want to see him again. I don't. I still don't.

I want to erase every memory of him from my mind. If only memories were drawn in pencil, life would be so much easier.

I want to forget the sound of his voice. The dirty words that fall from his lips. The easy touches. His powerful influence. The way he treats my body like it's more than just a tool for his own pleasure… The way he treats his as it's a tool for *mine.*

I want to forget the way his tie felt wrapped around my wrists and the way his wicked tongue felt as it flicked across my clit.

I want to forget the way it felt to be perched on my desk with his fingers inside as I all but rode his hand to my own orgasm.

More than anything… I want to forget how badly I wanted those things the second I was presented with them.

I have Carter Hughes on the brain, and it's deadly.

My phone buzzes with a new message, and I type in my unlock code. It's from Carter telling me he's waiting outside, so I take a deep breath and slide my feet back into my beloved heels. My pencil skirt is tight, and I picked it deliberately this morning to hamper the efforts of wayward body parts.

Not that I truly believe a bit of black fabric will stop him if that's where he ultimately wants to be, but I'll definitely make it harder than it needs to be.

Harder than it needs to be. It's taking all my self-restraint not to giggle at myself right now.

God, I need food.

And wine. Definitely wine.

Wine is what I think about as I travel down in the elevator. It settles the butterflies in my tummy and stops my adrenaline kicking in too much.

My heels click across the lobby as I head for the door. I can already see him leaning against another sleek black car, wearing his trademark white shirt and black pants. His sleeves are rolled up, his tie nowhere to be seen, and his top two buttons undone.

I wish he didn't look so fucking hot like that.

He turns his face and our eyes meet. His seem even greener than I remember, if that's possible, and a shiver teases its way through my body. The hairs on my body stand on end as he pushes off of the car and walks to the door. He beats me to it by a split second and pulls it open with a smile that would drop the panties of a nun. "Ms. Donnelly," he greets me in a low voice.

"Mr. Hughes," I respond in kind, my voice stronger than I feel.

"Shall we?" He releases the door and motions toward the car.

I suppose we must. "Please." I follow him toward the vehicle where he once again gets the door for me.

I hate the way my heart beats double-time for the few seconds it takes me to get in.

"How was your trip?" I ask politely when the car starts moving.

"It was… hot." He smiles. "It went well, thank you. It's due to open next month and everything seems to be on track. Well, if you don't count the fact we need to find a new chef, but I'll send Julia out there next week to do that."

"Sounds like you have everything under control."

His eyes flash. "I'm always in control."

"Ah, yes. You're a control freak."

"Takes one to know one." He winks, grinning.

I'm not even going to respond to that.

"How are things here?" he asks, apparently sensing that he can't bait me that easily today.

"I stopped by an hour ago. The flooring is down, the wallpaper up, and the lights are being fitted. The new bar is being crafted so installation can begin tomorrow, then it's simply finalizing the delivery date for the tables and chairs."

"You're very efficient, Ms. Donnelly. I like that."

I turn my face toward him, arching one eyebrow. "I pride myself on my efficiency. Besides, the quicker this job is done, the quicker my life returns to its formerly Carter-less way."

He rests his arm across the back of the seat and leans forward. "Sounds like you can't wait to get rid of me, Bee."

I make sure to hold his gaze steadily as I respond. "I can't." I finish with a smile.

"Cute," he murmurs. He reaches forward and takes a lock of my hair. He twirls it around his finger gently, his eyes cutting to where the dark strands are sliding across his skin. He takes more hair, then more, and more, until half of it is gripped in his palm and he's leaning right into me.

My heart skips a beat as he moves my face closer to his. Our breath mingles in the small space between us, and I have shivers everywhere. The goosebumps that coat my skin contradict my earlier words.

His lips curl into a knowing half-smile. "What makes you think you can get rid of me that easily?"

"A stiletto through your balls?"

His chuckle is low and dark. "Oh, Bee." He slides across the seat and our thighs brush. I take a deep breath in. "I've missed your smart mouth these past three days."

"Really? All you had to do was call. I have a special amount of snark reserved for you."

"I'm sure you do." He releases his grip on my hair and eases back. He touches his thumb to the corner of my mouth and runs it across my lower lip, tugging on it softly. "Actually, I think I just missed your mouth in general. It's my favorite part of you."

"You're crossing the line again, Carter."

"What line would that be? The one you insisted be drawn? The very same one you can't keep to?"

"I'd keep to it if you'd stop touching me."

"And that's the problem, isn't it? You're standing on the edge of the line just waiting for me to join you there. You're hardly pushing me away, are you?"

No, and I don't want to. God help me, I don't.

"Exactly," he whispers, his voice husky. "Face it, Bee. There's never been a line. Not between us. You know that if I wanted to tug your skirt up and drag you on top of me, you wouldn't do a thing to stop it, would you?" He trails his hand across my side and cups my breast. "If I took off your shirt and removed your bra, would you stop me taking your nipple in my mouth?"

My breathing picks up.

"No? What about if I unbuttoned my pants and tugged your face down to my cock? Would you refuse?"

I lick my lips.

"Stop fooling yourself." He pushes the hair back from my eyes. His strong gaze flickers across my face, studying every one of my features, before he finally catches mine. "You fight this because you can't control it. You fight it because that's the only way you can control it. But make no mistake, Bee, if I wanted you on your knees in front of me, you know that's exactly where you'd be, because you know you'd want it as badly as me."

My chest is heaving with each desperate breath I take, and I know his game. His cards are on the table, face up, and he isn't even trying to hide them.

That's fine.

I want to play too.

I trail my fingers up his chest and let them rest against the side of his neck. "And what if I stopped fighting it and did control it? Would you stop me?" I tuck my legs beneath me and push him back on the chair. I dip my face so my hair falls around us in a dark curtain. He slides his hand down my back and across my ass cheek.

He wastes no time pulling it back then smacking it with a serious amount of force. "You wouldn't be in control, baby. Don't think you would be."

"Really? Because I beg to differ." I drop my face so our lips touch, but there's no kissing in the movement. Just a gentle hover. "What if," I whisper, "What if I pushed you on your back right now, hiked up my skirt, and crawled up your body so my pussy was right over your face? Are you telling me you wouldn't slide my panties to the side and lick it, Carter? Are you honestly telling me that'd be you in control? Or if I reached down right now and pulled your cock out and climbed on top of you to fuck you. Who'd be in control then?"

His fingers dig into my ass, and his other hand scoops my hair up and tugs.

Hard.

He yanks my head back and grazes his teeth down my neck. "Who's in control now, Bee? Now who has who where they want them? Because the way I see it, you can't move."

I drop my hand and cup his cock. I can feel its hard length pushing against the material of his pants, and I run a nail along it, right next to the zipper. "Fifty-fifty, *baby.*"

"Touché," he responds, swirling his tongue across the exposed curve of my neck. "There is a difference though, isn't there?"

"There is?" I ask breathlessly.

He pushes my head forward quickly and my eyes flutter shut. His lips brush over mine. "Yeah. My control is very, very fucking close to snapping. So behave yourself, Bee. Because the place I know that does great food also delivers, and it's already waiting for us."

My eyes open quickly. "Where?"

His lips curve up with the knowledge he has me cornered. "In my fucking kitchen."

Oh, boy.

———◦◦◦◦◦◦———

I honestly wish I'd insisted on meeting him in a restaurant. I don't care if this house is huge and immaculately decorated, or if the rustic charm of the kitchen had me sighing with happiness as I stepped through the door.

My pussy is wet, my nipples are aching, and my clit is considering a petition for release.

Still, I'm sitting at the island counter in the middle of Carter's majestic kitchen, my chin propped up in my hand, waiting for him to unpack our lunch.

Many things are wrong with this situation. The first being is that he decided to remove his shirt and throw it over one of the chairs opposite me. So I'm sitting here trying to refrain from giggling like a sixteen year old as the muscles in his back flex with his every morning.

Seriously. Backs. Sexy as fuck. Why? Who knows? Who cares?

I'm trying to think of something—of anything, that will take my mind off this whole situation I'm in. It isn't working. It's so screwed up. I should have told him hell no the second he told me we were here. He couldn't have forced me in, could he?

No… He's an asshole, but he doesn't have the whole kidnapping credentials. Although I'm sure if he really wanted to, he could finish me off and hide my body without another thought.

Oh God.

Mayday. Mayday.

"Wine?"

I squeak as I focus on him.

His lips curve on one side. "Am I interrupting a sordid fantasy?"

"Does you killing me and hiding my body count as one?"

"No."

"Then, no."

He stares at me for a moment then holds up a bottle of pink wine. "Wine?" he repeats.

No. "Please."

Dammit, brain.

He pours a glass and sits it in front of me, then turns and produces a plate full of Caesar salad. My eyes narrow, but I quickly return my expression to normal as I thank him and gets his own. He takes the seat opposite me, all rippling muscle, and grabs his wine glass. "To a successful project."

"To a successful project," I echo, much softer than he spoke. He sips his wine and sets the glass down. I, meanwhile, take a mouthful and left the fruity taste linger on my tongue for a few seconds before swallowing.

Carter doesn't say a word as he picks up his cutlery and eats. I drop my eyes, get my fork, and stab it into a piece of chicken. It smells really good, but honestly, I'm not sure if I'm even hungry anymore. I'm still reeling from our exchange in our car, and if I'm honest with myself, I'm more embarrassed than anything. I rarely speak to anyone like that, and if I do, I sure as hell never see them again.

Now here I am, sitting in his kitchen, eating lunch with him. In a suspiciously quiet working lunch meeting.

It feels horribly comfortable.

You know that sensation when you go somewhere you feel like you've been before or that you should be? That kind of comfort. It's as if I've been here a thousand times or are destined to be here that many.

It's unnerving. It doesn't have a place in my world, yet I have an inexplicable need to set down my fork and explore every possible nook and cranny of this gorgeous house. I want to browse every bookshelf and open every cupboard and run my hand over every wall.

And I wish I could say it's from the perspective of an interior designer—it isn't.

It's from the perspective of something I don't want to think about.

Carter takes another sip from his glass and nods to my plate. "Something wrong with it?"

"Oh, no." I glance up at him then back at my plate. "I just don't feel particularly hungry."

With the glass still in his hand, he fixes his gaze on me. I know because I can feel it—it's as obvious as an icy blast of air at the height of summer. "You keep looking at the door."

"The hallway," I admit. "I kind of want to explore. Your house looks gorgeous."

He reaches for a paper napkin from the stack and wipes the corner of his mouth. "You want a tour?"

"Oh—you don't have to. I'm being rude." I smile slightly and push a slice of chicken around my plate.

"Grab your glass." He grins and gets up, his in hand. "Come on."

I hesitate for a second too long, and he rounds the island. He grabs my hand and pulls me up, then releases me just to deposit my wine glass in my palm. "I guess I'll come, then," I say quietly, fighting my smile.

"Are you ready for the grand tour of Casa de Hughes?" he asks, walking backward out of the kitchen. His eyes fall to my feet and he holds out a hand to stop me. "Woah, woah. Those weapons have gotta come out of your feet. We have fifteen rooms to explore and there's no way you can do that in those animals."

"Those animals—"

"Cost more than a pedigree puppy, yeah, yeah. I know. Still. Off." He stands in front of me until I sigh with resignation and bend down to pull them off my feet.

Safely off, I kick them to the side and meet his eyes. "There. Better?"

He grins and lifts his hand to the top of my head. "Wow. Those things are deceiving."

"You realize I'm at the right height to do this, don't you?" I lift one knee up.

He steps back. "Point made." Our gaze hovers for a moment, both of us smiling, then he turns. "First stop on the Grand Tour of the Hughes House is the dining room that has been used approximately one point five times in the last two years."

"One point five? How is that possible?"

"Once for Thanksgiving right after I moved in, then the following year when my mom designated me as the cook and I gave up after the turkey didn't show up."

"How does a turkey not show up?"

"I forgot to order it." He grimaces. "That was the first year she told me I need a woman. I reminded her I have her and my sister, and that's enough woman for anyone."

I laugh quietly, looking around the room. "It's dark in here."

"Yeah. I keep meaning to do something with it, but like I said, it doesn't get used." He shrugs and closes the door.

My eye twitches. Oh boy, I want to take my camera and sketch pad in there.

"And the living room." He opens the next door to a reasonably sized room about as well kitted out as can be expected for a man's living room. Dark-colored sofas, a giant television, games consoles, you name it, it's there. What I am surprised to see is an array of photos lining the exposed brick fireplace and even the windowsill. I really want to go forward and look, but I manage to stop myself. "And what my sister jokes is my bedroom, living room and dining room all in one, my office." He opens a door across the hall and takes me into the biggest room I've been in.

It is literally massive. There's a sectional sofa at one end complete with coffee table. A sprawling desk with comfortable leather chair. Shelves of reference books, including many cookery books, and stacks upon stacks of folders.

"You have recipe books," I say slowly, reaching for one and pulling it from the shelf.

"I own restaurants."

"But you forget to order Thanksgiving turkey?"

"Fuck," he hisses. "I hate cooking, all right? I can make cereal and that's it."

"You don't make cereal. You put it in a bowl and pour milk on top of it."

"You're starting to ruin my elusive manner here, Bee."

"You? Elusive? Not on your life, Carter Hughes. You're as elusive as wasp around a group of teenage girls."

His eyebrows arches in the way I'm rapidly becoming familiar with. "Mysterious?"

"Not so mysterious either," I lie. "You're like an orange just waiting to be peeled open."

"That's the oddest thing I've ever been called," he muses. "Come on. There's upstairs yet. Unless you want to see the spare rooms."

Upstairs? Wait. I didn't consider upstairs did I? "What's in the spare rooms?"

"Absolutely nothing," he admits.

"Then I'm good."

He grins, and there's something suggestive about it. "Upstairs?"

"I think I'm good." I lift my wine glass to my lips.

"Bee... I can fuck you anywhere. The desk. The sofa. The wall. Taking you upstairs really isn't going to make a difference."

I cough, swallowing my wine wrong. "No, no, I got that," I croak out, patting my chest. "I was just... Well. I don't need to see upstairs."

Carter tilts his head to one side and studies me. His bright green gaze is unnerving, and I shudder under his gentler-than-usual scrutiny. "All right," he says slowly. "No bedrooms. Another room. If I've got you figured out, Bee Donnelly, I sense you'll appreciate it."

"What is it? Like a spa or something?"

He laughs, holding out his hand. My eyes narrow, and I glance at his hand. He makes a 'come here' motion with his fingers, not moving any closer to me.

"How do I know you're not going to drag me into your bedroom and have your way with me?"

"If I planned on that, your skirt would already be around your hips and my cock would be buried inside you," he answers matter-of-factly. "And yes, I understand we have yet to get to your important business, but I'm curious."

I swallow. "Curiosity killed the cat, Mr. Hughes."

"Then I must be the cat, and you the curiosity, Ms. Donnelly," he responds in a low voice, stepping toward me. My heart thuds. "Because I'm damn sure you're gonna kill me."

"All right," I whisper. "Show me how well you think you know me."

And then I place my hand in his.

CHAPTER TEN

*C*arter's fingers close around mine. He tugs me out of the room and toward the winding staircase. As we go up it, I realize it's a gentle spiral, and both the little girl in my soul and the designer in my heart sing their way up to it. If I weren't holding my wine glass, my fingers would be brushing the gorgeous wooden banister that follows the curve of the stairs. As it is, I settle for my eyes running along it.

At the top, we come to a spacious hallway, much barer than the rest of the house. Unlike downstairs, the doors are all open up here, and I can spy four bedrooms, two bathrooms, and a room I can't quite make out.

"The master bedroom with its private bath and walk-in closet are at the end of the hall," Carter tells me, motioning toward it with his glass. "The others are all spares—I keep them for my family. Mom lives in California and comes to visit every couple of months," he explains. "But that's not what I want to show you."

"I'm starting to think you really do have a sex chamber with whips and chains on the walls," I say hesitantly, looking at the slightly ajar oak door behind him.

He laughs. Loudly. Still holding his wine glass, he touches one finger to my lips. "I think the lady reads too much."

"There's no such thing as reading too much. That's like saying someone breathes too much."

"I have to agree."

His words surprise me, but not as much as what's behind the door does.

Oh, my heart.

I can't help the gasp that leaves my mouth. Oak bookshelves line two of the walls, built around the windows on the outside wall. Those small, square areas let an abundance of natural light into the room, and that light falls on the two huge couches that surround the fireplace right in the middle of it all. The open-brick chimneystack is stunning, offsetting the rich oak perfectly. The deep red rug that sits in the center of the dark brown sofas, peppered with red and cream cushions, is a stunning burst of color.

My hand falls from Carter's as I step past him and into the room.

Books.

Shelves.

Everywhere.

"This is nothing like the rest of the house," I breathe. "It's amazing."

"It isn't much," he says, following me in. "Izzy loves to read, and the first time she came here, she told me in very colorful language that it was sacrilege that I had a house this size without a library." He shakes his head. "She's a walking fairytale, my sister. Still, I had this put in. I believe she slept in here for two days the first time she saw it."

"I don't blame her." I run my fingertips along a shelf, and he steps up behind me. Without a word, he takes the wine glass from my hand, and I can't even thank him I'm so amazed.

He has the classics—all of them. American and British. The stories that are the very core of mystery and romance and adventure. Pure escapism within the pages that are bound by thick, leather covers.

That's all books are. Escapism borne of wonderfully crafted words that describe far off lands. Sentences that ask and answer within seconds. Paragraphs that slay dragons and ride horses into the midnight sky. Chapters that describe the sensation of pounding hearts and consuming desire, each feeling chronicling the incredible sensation of falling in love.

I run my fingers along the spines of each book, old and new, classic and modern, as I walk the length of the room. The shelves are ceiling high, each one filled and overflowing.

"It's a Belle library," I sigh, ducking down to the shelf below.

"A Belle library?" Carter questions, putting both wine glasses on the coffee table.

"In Beauty and the Beast? The ladder?"

"Ohh. That." He tilts his head to the side. "I guess so."

"It's amazing." I smile. "Good job."

His eyes are on me for the split second it takes him to cross the room. "I knew it," he says to me.

"Knew what?" I look up at him, my lips pulling into a small smile.

"You're an orange waiting to be peeled," he throws my own words back at me. "And I think I just did it."

Slowly, I stand, keeping my eyes on him. "I don't get it."

"You." He pushes some hair from my eyes, his fingers lingering on the side of my face. "The night we met, you made it so clear you don't want commitment. Why?"

"Why don't you?"

"That's not the conversation we're having."

"We're not having any conversation."

"You're a romantic at heart, aren't you, Bee? You're not so different to everyone else."

"I have no idea where you're going with this conversation," I breathe, stepping back. "What does who I am inside have to do with you, Carter? Your aversion to commitment is stronger than mine."

"I have an aversion to relationships because women tend to look at me and see a meal ticket. They see diamonds and expensive things and flash cars and vacations. I'm not averse to commitment, Bee. I'm simply averse to it with the wrong woman. That doesn't make a commitment-phobe. That makes me smart."

"Maybe I'm averse to commitment with the wrong guy. I hardly need someone to depend on and look after me, but I don't want someone that needs to depend on me."

"I know what's inside these pages. I may never have read them, but look." He pulls one from the shelf. "*Pride and Prejudice*. Everyone knows how that ends. Eventually the pride and prejudice doesn't matter and love prevails." He puts it back on the shelf and pulls out *Jane Eyre*. "Eventually Jane and Mr. Rochester fall in love." He replaces that and walks past me to a shelf with more modern books.

"*Fifty Shades of Grey.* Ana and Christian. They fall in love. *Cinderella. Rapunzel.* All the classic fairytales, Bee. They all end in love and happily ever after."

"Make your point, Carter, because I don't see it."

He pushes the gray book back into its place and walks to me. He stops, right in front of me, towering over me by several inches. "Maybe," he says, gently touching his hand to the side of my face. "Maybe you're less about the aversion and more about the dream."

I push his hand away. "And maybe you have no idea."

His green eyes are piercing. And they do. Pierce. Right down to my bones, to my very soul; the same soul that's yelling at me for arguing what I know to be so very true.

I believe in love. True love. Whirlwind, consuming love. I believe it exists for everyone, and I'll be damned if I'll settle for anything less.

He's right.

My aversion to commitment is more about a dream of what could be, more than anything else.

"Ever thought that one day you could be so averse to what's in front of you that you could skip right over what you want?" Carter asks, closing the distance between us once more. "That could be so wrapped up in perfection that you'll never appreciate flaws?"

"Okay, you've met my mother, and you've seen my office. There are flaws all up in that shit," I respond, snorting. "This... is getting out of hand. Can we just go eat now?"

He shakes his head. "I'm still the cat. I wanna know."

"Really? You wanna know why I'm holding out for the person that's right for me?"

"That seems like a pretty apt description of what I wanted to know, actually."

"Because there are too many people like you in the world, Carter." I flatten my hands against my stomach and take a deep breath. "Too many people that can manipulate your thoughts and your feelings until you believe everything to be true."

His smile drops. "That's what you think I'm doing? You think I'm fucking manipulating you?"

"Do I think that, when I'm done with your restaurant, we'll honestly never see each other again? Yes. I do. Totally. I know nothing about you, yet you make me feel a way I haven't in a long time. You make me feel a hundred different ways that I shouldn't."

"Elaborate," he demands, his eyes sparking. "If you think I'm manipulating you, tell me exactly how I make you feel and see how I respond."

"Wanted," I say quietly. "You make me feel wanted—and you make me believe that I am, too."

"That's because you are," he growls. "I want you, Bee. Fuck—I want you more than anything. How can you think that isn't true? It's taking everything I have not to grab you and show you that's true."

"Then do it," I challenge him, raising my chin. "Right now. Prove it. If you think you're a fucking romance hero and you really want me, show me."

"You have no idea what you're asking me to do," he warns me in a low voice. "I don't take this shit lightly, baby. I'm an asshole, but I'm not a user. If I have to show you how much I want you, I'll be fucking damned if I can take that back."

"I don't care," I return bravely. "I'm not a fucking pushover. I'm not a toy or a doll that can be stashed in a drawer or a cupboard until you're ready for another play. You just stood in front of me and you told me that you want a woman who doesn't look at you and see dollar signs. Newsflash, Carter, I don't see that. I see an asshole, but I see one who makes believe I'm wanted."

His jaw tightens, his eyes darkening.

"Prove it to me right now, or I'm walking out of that door, and believe me when I say you'll never see me again."

His movements are like a flash of lightning.

His hands in my hair. The bookshelves digging into my back. His bare chest against me. My lips crushed beneath him.

I can taste the lust on his lips.

It's intoxicating.

The kiss is everything. It's the verbal affirmation of the very thing I just demanded he prove, and I'm drowning beneath his determination. I'm drowning in his desperate exploration of my mouth.

"Believe it yet?" he rasps against me. "Believe that I'm not fucking lying to you when I tell you I want you?"

I stare into his eyes defiantly. "Kissing wasn't what I meant."

"Not all fairytales end as expected. Not everyone has a prince inside them."

"Belle never fell in love with the prince. She fell in love with the Beast."

He holds my gaze for one long, torturous minute, and then tugs me away from the shelves. His hand tightens around mine and he tugs me after him down the hall toward the master bedroom.

He kicks the door shut behind him, and I can barely register the blue and gray color scheme before he's spinning me and grasping my waist. He clasps the zipper at the back and undoes it, then pushes on the waistband. It falls to my feet, and he grabs the hem of my blouse.

My heart is on double-time. My lungs are demanding oxygen quicker than I can breathe it in. I'm tingling everywhere as anticipation dances across my skin. I can barely control myself as Carter's deft fingers work the buttons of my blouse until its undone and falling off my shoulders. Or maybe he's pushing it off. I don't know anymore. It's feeling after feeling and each one is stronger than the last.

He stands in front of me, and I force my eyes from his chest, up along the stubbled line of his jaw and the chiseled ridge of his cheekbone to where his eyes are focused intently on me. His look is chilling yet heated at the very same time, and I suck my lower lip into my mouth.

His gaze drops as I release it, dragging my teeth across it as I do so.

As if that movement were a switch, Carter snaps.

His hands dive back into my hair, and in the same movement, he kisses me. His lips are hungry as they move across mine, and I grasp his sides to keep standing as he walks with me. The backs of my calves hit the bed and we fall in a tangle of limbs and dueling tongues.

Need rushes through me, and I grasp at his back as he covers my body with his.

This is nothing like the first time.

That was fun. Easy. Playful.

This is carnal. Raw. Desperate.

And dammit, as he pulls back and I gasp for air as his mouth travels down my neck, my heart pounds a little harder—for him.

Not for the lust. Not for the sex. Not for the undeniable feeling of being wanted. But for the man—whom I hardly know—that's making me feel all these things.

And there isn't a damn thing I can do about it.

Carter tugs away my bra and immediately closes his mouth around one of my nipples. His tongue traces shapes over the hardened point as his thumb does the same to my other. Fuck me. It's like they have a direct line to my clit. I'm hyper sensitive of every movement he makes as he switches his mouth to the other side and slides his hand down my body.

My skin burns wherever he touches me. It's like every fingerprint he leaves behind is a flaming ring of fire that brands me. His mouth is the same. The teasing trail of kisses he peppers down my stomach as he leans back onto his knees has me writhing beneath him.

As his hands travel down, his fingers loop in the sides of my underwear and slide them down my legs. I bend my knees, and his grasp from panties to thighs is immediate. He wraps his arms around my thighs, holding my legs wide open, and yanks me down the bed.

His mouth is on me before I've had a chance to gasp, and holy fuck, yes, his mouth is on me.

His wicked tongue works my clit. Flicking and circling and rubbing with each kiss he covers my pussy with. I can't stand the assault he's unleashing on me, and I go from my hands in my hair, to grasping sheets, to winding my fingers in his hair. The only sound in the room is of my heavy breathing, interspersed with my helpless moans.

It feels so good.

He lets me go as abruptly as he took hold of me and stands. I run my fingers through my hair, my chest heaving. I manage to look down in time to see him stepping out of his pants and boxers and leaning over. The sound of a drawer opening and closing breaks through my breaths, and Carter leans over me, a shiny foil packet in his hand.

His eyes are bright, but there's a darkness hinting in their depths. It intrigues me and excites me at the same time, especially when he rips the condom packet open with his teeth. His gaze never falters as he spits the corner of the packet out to the side and pulls out the rubber inside. He stands, and I bite down on the inside of my cheek as he takes his long, hard cock and rolls the condom over it.

There is something stupidly sexy about watching a man touch himself, even if he's just putting on protection.

In fact. That is the fucking sexy part.

He scoops one arm behind my knee as he falls back down, bending my leg right up. My thigh is as flat against my stomach as it can go, and he lifts my butt, leaning over me until his cock brushes my wet pussy. "Believe me now?" he rasps into my ear. He slides his hand into my hair and cups the back of my head. "Did I lick your pussy enthusiastically enough for you, baby?"

I nod and push my hips down as far onto his cock as I can. His low, devilish chuckle makes me tremble even harder.

I know it's coming, but I still cry out anyway.

My pussy aches as it stretches to accommodate his large cock, and I grasp desperately at his back and shoulders as he waits it out. "God," I whisper.

"Not my name but I'll take it," he laughs quietly, tightening his grasp on my leg. "Fuck, Bee." He eases out of me and back in again. "I fucking love your pussy."

Fuck yeah, I like her right now, too.

He pulls my face up and kisses me and picks up the pace of his thrusts. Heat swamps me as the teasing of his tongue and the deep strokes of his cock inside me combine together in a deadly hit that feels like it should be some kind of a dream.

Each kiss gets harder.

Each moan louder.

Each thrust deeper.

I'm spiraling out of control as we move together. I don't even know if I am moving. I think it's all him. I think it's just Carter, pounding into me, tilting my hips up and down and sideways and arching my back and nipping my lower lip and chuckling into my ear. I think he's doing everything, but that's because all I know is him.

All I can see, smell, taste, feel, hear… It's him. Just him.

He releases me, pulling out of me, and flips me onto my front with no effort at all. I reach around the back of my neck and sweep my hair to one side so I can look at him.

With a wickedly sexy grin on his face, he pushes me onto my knees, then slaps one hand across my ass. I flinch as the sweet sting travels across my skin and prop myself onto my elbows.

He wastes no time spreading my ass cheeks and pushing his cock back into my pussy. He's deeper here, and I bury my face in the covers as my body convulses with pleasure. I feel him, rather than see him, as he leans fully forward. His hot breath skitters across my ear as he says, "Do I want you enough now, Bee?"

I nod. Yes. I feel it. I believe it.

Now I want all of it.

I clench my pussy around him. He hisses out a long breath and straightens again. "I'll take that as a yes." He slaps my ass right before he slams into me and a breathy moan falls from my lips.

Those are the last words he says as he focuses on drawing every last bit of pleasure from me.

And draw it he does.

My orgasm barrels into me, an impossibly strong force, and I surrender to it.

I barely register Carter's as my own consumes me. He buries himself inside me, his words and groans nothing but murmurs to me as my blood thunders through my ears.

We roll to the side, and I push my hair from my face to breathe clearly. He settles his arm over my waist as he catches his breath, then props himself up on his elbow. "You didn't have another appointment this afternoon, did you?" he asks me, amused.

"Nope… But I am supposed to be at the restaurant again," I respond, smiling back at him.

"I'm pretty sure your client won't mind." He cups my chin and kisses me softly. "Wait here." He pulls out of me and removes the condom, then disappears into the bathroom to the side of the room.

A chill skates across my skin now he isn't here, and my stomach ties itself into a knot.

Wait here? Like this? Naked on his bed like he's going to draw me like a fucking French girl? Uh, no. That's not how this works.

Hell, nothing is working like any of it is supposed to at this point.

I sit up and grab the covers, pulling them back and over me. It chases away the slight coldness and makes me feel a bit more… appropriate, let's say.

Sure, Bee. You just came all over your client's cock, *in his bed,* but let's think about appropriateness *now.*

Shit.

Carter comes out of the bathroom and throws me a towel. He's walking around with absolutely nothing on, his cock still semi-hard, but that doesn't seem to faze him as he pulls open a drawer to his dresser and removes some underwear.

I clean up awkwardly as he puts his boxers on, then I reach forward and grab my panties. My unwearable panties.

He turns and his eyes drop to the underwear I'm holding. "Ah."

"There's, uh… A spare pair in my purse."

His eyes snap up to mine, dancing with laughter. "There is, is there?"

I lift a shoulder. "You told me to bring spare panties. What can I say? Sometimes I do as I'm told." Especially when there's a chance it could benefit me.

He winks and heads out of the room. I watch, unashamedly, as he walks away. I mean, come on. I pretty much just screamed whatever shame I had left right on out of my body.

And talking of shame…

The real shame should be that I haven't done what I was supposed to do when I came here. Shit. Fuck. I just let him seduce me and get under my skin even more than he already is. Now I'm afraid he's kind of stuck there.

He is, isn't he?

Oh, God. Of all the people to get stuck under my skin, it had to be him.

Talking of him… He comes back into his room, holding my purse. I crack a smile at seeing this handsome, six-foot something, ripped as hell man wearing black and white boxer briefs, carrying a bright red Michael Kors purse.

"My color?" he questions, swinging it over his shoulder and pouting.

A laugh bursts out of me.

This cannot be real.

"You didn't have to bring the whole thing," I tell him, taking it and setting it on my lap. I locate my panties fairly quickly.

"You never go in a ladies' purse," Carter laughs quietly. "I told you—I was raised a gentleman. And that includes the spanking."

I want to roll my eyes, but what I actually do is run my tongue over my teeth. I grab my bra and get dressed, locating my blouse on the floor at the end of the bed. I slip my arms in and my fingers are poised to do up the first button when Carter approaches me.

He crooks two fingers beneath my chin and gently tilts my head up. His eyes are like an amazing emerald beacon, and my gaze is drawn to them instantly. "No snarky comeback? No smart-mouthed dig?"

I open my mouth to respond, but settle for shaking my head.

"What's wrong?"

My teeth graze over my bottom lip. "You told my mom about us."

He stills. "Was that the reason for this urgent meeting?"

"Yes. I'm… well, I was mad at you. I think you successfully fucked that right out of me." I step away from him and do up two of my buttons before turning back to him and resting my hands on my hips. "Why would you do that?" He holds his hands up, but before he can say a word, I carry on. "Do you have any idea how fucking embarrassed I was when she told me? I've barely spoken to her for three days, Carter! Fucking hell—I may be a grown woman and able to make my own choices and mistakes, but I never once felt the need to bring what happened between us two weeks ago into your business decision!"

"Mistake?" he growls. He stalks toward me and grasps my chin, his eyes blazing down at me. "First things first. Did that feel like a fucking mistake to you, Bee? 'Cause it sure as hell didn't to me."

I lick my lips in lieu of an answer.

First time was a mistake. The second? Totally deliberate.

"And second, I didn't tell your mom a damn thing. I told her we knew each other through a mutual friend, and *that* was the mistake. She assumed—correctly—that we had a closer relationship than I was letting on, because why else would I tell her?"

"That is an excellent question," I grind out, knocking his arm back.

"For you," he says, taking the hand that just hit him. "Because even that night, I knew you were a feisty little thing. I wanted your mom to know that the only reason I hired you is because I couldn't not, because you're that goddamn fucking good at your job that there was never another option for a designer. I didn't want her to find out somehow, someday, that you and I had been together and think that was the reason I hired you. I didn't want anyone to find out and think of that, because you're too damn good to be looked at as a pity case, Bee Donnelly."

I take a deep breath in at those words. My throat is dry, and I lick my lips yet again in an attempt to create some saliva. "You didn't need to hire me. Someone else could—"

"Not have done that design. You just… saw it. The others were good, don't think I'm discrediting them. They were real fucking good, but they weren't yours. Somehow you took what I envisioned and put it on paper without even asking me. How? I don't know. I don't want to know. I just know that in that moment nothing mattered more than it being abundantly clear that your skills as a designer were why I hired you."

"Okay," I say quietly. "Thank you. For doing that."

He rubs his thumb over my pulse point, and with his other hand, brushes the back of his fingertips over my cheek. "You're very welcome."

I nod and avert my gaze. "What do we do now? I mean… What is this, Carter? What just happened?"

He inhales sharply and dips his face down to mine. My eyes flutter shut as our noses touch. "I don't know, baby," he rumbles. "But I like it. And I wanna keep it if you do."

Do I? Want to keep this? "Keep it for what?"

"Trust me when I say I would have found you even if that Monday morning meeting wasn't rescheduled with you. You intrigued me enough. There're only a days left of the renovations. Spend that time with me. Let's see where it goes."

"In four days?"

He raises his eyebrows. "Cinderella fell in love in one night. We could be married in four days."

I jerk back and stare at him. "I seriously hope you're kidding right now."

He looks at me, stony faced, and just when I'm about to tell him exactly what I think of that bullshit idea, he bursts out laughing and pulls me against him. "You bet your hot ass I'm fucking kidding. Marriage." He shudders.

"Good to see we still agree on something," I mutter as he lets me go. "Uh, Carter?"

"What?"

"You know we can't tell anyone we're spending time together... right? My mom is kind of trusting me not to do what just happened while you're still technically a client."

He rests a forearm on the dresser and meets my eyes across the room. "Thought you said you were good at doing what you were told."

I pick up my skirt and smile sweetly.

He shakes his head and turns away.

Whoopsie.

CHAPTERELEVEN

*T*he walls are done. The floors are done. The bar area is almost complete.

It's starting to resemble something that doesn't look like a hurricane whipped through it.

I walk to the bar and grip the plastic surrounding the glass top, then tug. The creaks of it as I pull the coating away are oddly satisfying.

"So… what does that mean, exactly?" Charley asks, walking to the other side of the bar. "You'll 'see where it goes?'"

I shrug. "I'm kinda hoping it'll end up in bed, and that's about it."

"So why agree?" She catches a bit of plastic that's still stuck to the bar with her nail and peels it off. "Why don't you just be fuck buddies?"

I don't answer. Honestly, I don't really have an answer. All I know is that, yesterday, in his room, in his house, after those deep conversations and sex, something made me agree. In fact, it barely crossed my mind not to agree.

Apparently I can be swayed by books and dirty, glorious sex.

Could be worse, I guess.

"You like him, don't you?" Charley asks, stopping.

I swat at her hand so she doesn't get the top of the bar covered in fingerprints. In hindsight, maybe leaving the plastic cover on was the better choice. "He's very charming."

"Charming? What are you? A romance heroine from the nineteenth century? Fuck!" She laughs, flicking her hair over her shoulder. "Charming my ass!"

"Fine!" I turn to her. "Yes, I like him, all right? He's fucking infuriating, but he makes me feel good. I'm learning more about him and he's not that much of a bad guy."

"Still think blind dates are a dumb idea?"

I glare at her.

She laughs. "He doesn't happen to have a brother, does he?"

"No, just a sister." I laugh back. "But I'm pretty sure she doesn't swing that way, and I know you sure as hell don't."

"Depends. For the right price I could."

"That's called porn." I snort and reach behind me for my purse. "I'm so ready for this to be done. It's so close now."

"What's left?" she asks, looking around. "Just furniture?"

"And a few other bits the builders are installing this afternoon. The restrooms are done apart from fresh flowers and a new mirror."

"You're getting antsy for something new, aren't you?" She smiles knowingly. "And perhaps knowing that you can spend time with your client when he isn't your client?" Her eyebrows waggle suggestively.

"That has nothing to do with it." Mostly nothing to do with it. "But, yeah. I'm dying for something new. Ten days feels like an age. This is why I stick to houses, mostly. Rooms don't take that long to redo."

"Well, you said yourself the dining room could do with some work." Carter's voice rumbles across the restaurant, and I look up to see him standing in the doorway between the bar and the restaurant. "Do you have a moment?"

"Sure." I turn to Charley. "I'll call you later?"

Her eyes flick between us. "Mhmm." She grabs her own purse from her feet and looks at Carter. "Nice to see you again, Carter."

"And you, Charley." The smile on his face reeks of amusement, and I wonder if he's trying to contain his laughter.

Charley gives me an 'ooh la la' kind of look, with her lips pouting and her eyebrows arched. I roll my eyes, smiling myself.

My best friend is bonafide crazy.

The door to the restaurant shuts, and Carter pushes off from the doorframe. "It looks good in here. Really good. I love the bar."

"It's my favorite part, too," I agree, running my finger along the rounded edge of it. "Looks much classier than that old thing you had in here before."

"You wound me," he teases, his hand flattened against his chest with mock drama. "Will you be here much now?"

"Most of the time." I drop my hand from the bar and meet his eyes. "I need to make sure the builders install everything correctly, and then the furniture will be here tomorrow. And trust me when I say I'm the one that needs to make sure that all goes in the right places."

"Really? I can't imagine why." His tone is dry, but laughter flickers in his gaze. "Do you need any help?"

"With what? The furniture? I guess."

"Good. Because my sister wants to come and see the restaurant… and meet you."

"Well, this went from blind date to what the fuck real quickly."

He pauses, then laughs deeply. "I'm choosing to go with her reasoning being you're the designer."

"Damn. You're better at this than me."

"I've had more time to practice. I'm older than you are."

"You make it sound like we're playing baseball or something."

"We kind of are," Carter rumbles, rounding the side of the bar and coming to me. He softly brushes some loose hairs from my face with his fingers. "All I know is that I want you, Bee. That's it."

My tongue darts out across my lower lip. "Do you think that's enough?"

"Dunno." He leans into me and brushes his lips across my jaw. "Is it for you?" He flicks his tongue against the tender spot beneath my ear.

I inhale sharply. Could want be enough—just want by itself?

I don't know, but it's a damn good start, isn't it?

"I think so," I breathe, my fingers brushing against his white shirt.

He pulls back and moves in to kiss me, but the moment is broken by the sound of his phone ringing from his pocket. He stills, sighs, then steps back. I laugh quietly and grab the folder containing my plans.

"Hello... Already?... Jesus, Izzy... I know that, but I thought you were coming tomorrow... I didn't say that, did that?... So sue me... All right, all right. I hear you... Yes, Izzy.... I said all right." He rubs his hand across his forehead and blows out a long breath. "I'll see you soon." He hangs up and slips his phone into his pocket, fixing me with a grim look.

"What's up?" I ask, glancing up at him.

"Remember how I said my sister would be stopping by?"

"Yes..."

"She'll be here in five minutes."

———◆◇◆◇◆———

This really has escalated kind of quickly.

It was one thing to know that she might stop by before he left for California, when Carter was nothing more than a bit of a mistake and a temptation to be overcome. Now, though...

God, sex changes everything, doesn't it?

It's a miracle I've used it so casually for so long. It's never made a difference to my life or affected me until Carter.

Maybe it isn't so much that sex changes everything.

Maybe he's the person who's changed everything. A chance meeting that lead to another, and eventually to where we are right now.

The worst part is that I don't know if I'd change it. I can't think of a scenario in which the last two or so weeks of my life would have been the same if we hadn't have slept together that night. I'm almost glad we did. I kind of want to hug my inner slut, because as crazy as it sounds, I can't help but feel like Carter understands me.

And really, we make quite a lot of sense, don't we? We're both independent. I don't see money or expensive things when I look at him because I have my own.

He doesn't look at me like someone who needs him to look after them, because he knows I can do that, too.

In a crazy twist of fate, we're so alike in what we want, that we're just about perfect for each other.

"Hellooooo?" a woman's voice sings out from the front door.

Carter and I turn at the same time. My first thought is that Carter lied, and she's actually his twin, because aside from the fact her features are more delicate than his and her hair is much longer, she looks exactly like him, even down to the stunning green eyes.

"Izzy." Carter walks to her and embraces her.

"Carter!" she squeals, hugging him back tightly. She releases him and looks around. "Ooooh, it's so much prettier here now!" Her eyes fall on me. "And you must be Bee!"

"That's me," I respond, a hint of shyness to my voice. "I've heard a lot about you."

"And I, you!" Izzy bounds over to me and wraps me in an enthusiastic hug. "It's so great to meet you!"

"Sorry," I hear Carter mutter. "I forgot to mention that she's an enthusiastic hugger."

I raise my eyebrows at him. "You think?" I mouth, taking a deep breath as she lets me go.

"Are these your plans from now? Can I see? He only showed me the basic ones." Izzy darts around my side and looks at the sheets spread out on the counter. "Ohhh, I love this." The sheets move around. "These are amazing. Holy shit, I'm sorry, I'm totally messing up your organization here."

Carter snorts. "Bee wouldn't know organization if it smacked her in the face."

"Hey! Organized chaos, remember?" I protest.

"Yeah, yeah. I remember."

"Carter! Don't be an asshole. I know that's hard for you to grasp, but try and be nice," Izzy admonishes him.

"All right. If you're pretending to be my big sister, I'm going to do some work." He rolls his shoulders and heads past us, throwing me a wink as he approaches the door.

"I won't judge if you kiss her," Izzy calls, looking a sheet of my design.

"Izzy," he warns her.

She rolls her eyes and nudges my arm. "He's an idiot."

"Isabel!"

CHAPTERTWELVE

"*You* have no idea how sorry I am for dumping my sister on you these last couple days."

I laugh at his apology. "You don't need to keep apologizing to me. I already told you—she's not bad company. Once she gets her excitement out of the way, at least."

To say Izzy Hughes is exhausting is somewhat of an understatement. She's twenty-six like me, but she has the endless energy of a room full of four year olds. There's always something to be talked about or laughed over or a joke to be told. I've slept so well the last few nights... Although that could also be the fact I've spent the last three nights with Carter and there's been more a little bit of sex.

He puts a plate of bacon and pancakes on the island in front of me, then gets his own and sits opposite em. He's wearing sweatpants and a t-shirt, and I love seeing him in this instead of his usual white shirt and black pants uniform. It's nice to see him as Carter the guy, instead of Carter the businessman.

"Were you serious about the dining room?" I ask him, reaching for orange juice. "Because I won't lie, I've pretty much not stopped thinking about that awful décor."

He looks up and grins while eating. He swallows, then speaks. "Sure. Go ahead. Just make sure to put a big ass fucking table in there, yeah?"

"Why do you need a big ass table? You told me you don't use it."

"So I can fuck you on it."

"Obviously. Why didn't I think of that?"

"Because you're probably thinking about damn wallpaper."

I pause, my fork hovering in front of my mouth, and look at him. Dammit. How did he know that? That isn't fair. "Shut up."

"Make me." His eyes twinkle with the challenge.

I hit the 'home' button on my phone. "Can't, sorry. I have to be at work in thirty minutes to finish up with the restaurant for my client's approval. I'd hate to be late and piss him off."

He groans. "You're right. Your client will be very pissed if it isn't finished today."

I smile. "My client is also still in his sweatpants."

"Your client can wear his sweatpants to work. It's why he's the boss." He winks, grins, and shovels the final piece of bacon into his mouth. "Now shall we get ready?"

"What do you mean, we? I'm ready. It's just you."

"Semantics, baby." He laughs and walks to me. He cups my face with his hands and drops a kiss onto my lips. "I will get ready. You go. I'll meet you at the restaurant to look it over, and then I'm taking you for dinner. *Out* someplace nice."

"Really?" My heart jumps.

"Bee, as soon as you've done your walkthrough and I've checked the restaurant, I'm no longer your client. And honestly, I don't care anymore. Anyone who can handle my sister like you do is not getting away from me."

"That's cute. I was under the impression getting away from you wasn't an option anyway."

"You are correct." He kisses me again.

"I was still going to attempt it, though. Just for the record."

He gives me the side-eye as he walks out of the kitchen, but his lips are turned up in a smirk.

I shoot him my sweetest smile.

I can't help but think that this seeing where it goes thing has really worked out. The last few days have been nothing but work, arranging the restaurant, and chilling out away from it all. Funny movies and TV shows have been broken up by random and impulsive sex sessions, but between it all, we've talked. We've got to know each other beyond it—we've peeled away each other's orange skins, as it is.

And I have to say, I'm finding that I like who Carter Hughes IS, more and more.

My dress skims my knees as I step out of the car, my hand in Carter's. "I thought you said we were going someplace nice," I tell him, looking at the restaurant in front of us.

"I have it on good authority that Carter's is one of the best in the business—and the owner is one hell of a fucking guy." He grins and leads me toward the door.

"This look is all yours, baby. I don't reopen until tomorrow. I thought we could enjoy it alone tonight."

"We're going to be skipping dinner, aren't we? I know your plan," I tell him as he leads me inside.

"You want to go straight to the back? I promise to feed you after this time."

"Oh so kind of you. I had to eat chips and salsa last time."

He laughs and pulls out a chair for me. It's the only table currently set fully, and a tea light candle is burning in the frosted glass holder I insisted every table needed. "Maybe you should eat first. Just in case."

I suck my lower lip into my mouth and consider my move. I could sit and we could have dinner, or I could take him to the back this time... I smile coyly at him. "Or maybe..." I spin and drag him toward the door that leads to the bar. "Maybe we can eat later."

I bump the bar door open with my butt, and Carter catches it with his free hand. His eyes darken, his smirk turning predatory, and it takes him all of a second to spin us and take control. I laugh as he pulls me along the bar, right back to the booth where it all started, and tugs me into it. I'm still laughing as I fall back onto the plush leather seat, and Carter swings the curtains shut before turning to me.

God, that smile.

He drops down over me, one knee sliding between my legs, and wraps one arm around the small of my back. "Before we go any further, two things."

"It's never good if you have to talk before sex," I mutter, running my nails up his sides and back down to his belt. I grip it tightly.

"Mmmm." He drops his lips. "I bought a club. With a friend."

"Congratulations. And I'm guessing you want to hire me again."

"Depends..." He trails his lips down my neck, and I arch my head back, closing my eyes. "Do we have to keep hiding this? 'Cause I won't lie, Bee... I don't want to hide you. I want you too badly to hide you anymore."

I gasp as he nips my neck. "No," I breathe, grabbing his shirt and untucking it. "No more hiding."

"Thank fuck." He slips his hand into my hair and pulls my mouth up to his. "You're mine."

My hands explore the smooth plains of his back. "Don't get too cocky now."

"Bee," he murmurs, one of his hands easing between my legs. "Your pleasure is mine. Your pussy is mine. You're mine. Is that clear?"

"As crystal. Now prove it."

"As you wish."

THEEND

Thank you for reading Blind Date, a novella! I hope you enjoyed it. For more information about me and any of my upcoming works, please join my reader group at http://bit.ly/EmmaHartsHartbreakers. I'd love to see you there!

BLIND DATE

ABOUT THE AUTHOR

Emma Hart is the *New York Times* and *USA Today* bestselling author of sexy new adult romance novels, including the Call series and the Game series. By day, she dons a cape and calls herself Super Mum to two beautiful little monsters. By night, she drops it, pours a glass of whatever she fancies—usually wine—and writes books.

Find Emma online at:

EmmaHart.org

Facebook.com/EmmaHartBooks.

@EmmaHartAuthor on Twitter and Instagram

@authoremmahart on Pinterest

Made in the USA
Coppell, TX
04 October 2024

38159898R00075